Lamella

Max Halper

Printed in the United States of America
First Edition: 2021
eBook ISBN 978-1-7355829-2-4
Softcover ISBN 978-1-7355829-1-7

Published By Bad Dream Entertainment®
www.BadDreamEntertainment.com

Cover Illustration by Dolce Paganne
Cover Design by Ia Gabunia
Final Manuscript Polish by Melissa Peitsch

The 'EyeBrain' logo is a registered trademark of Bad Dream Entertainment, Seattle, WA.
Original trademark design by Darcray

For Liv

"All sorts of things in this world behave like mirrors."
~Jacques Lacan

I came home and found my girlfriend on the sofa in the den, holding something.

"We missed you," she said.

I was preoccupied and flitted around the house, brooding about my day. One of my English 101 students had plagiarized his latest paper; when I failed him, he went to the administration to throw a fit. Now the administration had come to me, demanding proof of the plagiarism, which I could not provide other than to compare the student's previous written work—riddled with typos and grammatical issues—to this last paper, which was of a notably higher academic order. This apparently did not satisfy the school's criteria for a charge of plagiarism, and now *I* was the one suspected of impropriety. The whole thing was an asinine joke because there was hardly a question whatsoever that plagiarism had occurred. I barely even glanced at my girlfriend for a few minutes, until I managed to pause and take a breath. Which is when I noticed the thing she was holding.

"What is that?" I asked.

She smiled as if I was joking and adjusted the weight of the thing deeper into the crook of her arm. "Asleep, finally," she said. "I was starting to worry it wasn't going to happen." She got up and stood with her shoulder against my chest, and gazed down into the nest of blankets in her arms.

I followed her gaze and saw there, swathed in the dark pit of the blankets, something like a face— furrowed as if in some great reluctance, and pale like blank paper. I laughed somewhat incredulously, not getting the joke. The face rippled and knotted, the blankets stirred.

"Hush," my girlfriend hissed. "I just got her to sleep." She carried the thing gingerly up the stairs into the dark.

I was left standing in the den, blinking, preparing myself not to startle when everyone jumped out at me and went, "Gotcha!" with their cell phones out and everything. Though, of course, there was no one there, and nowhere for anyone to hide even if there was.

In the bedroom I found my girlfriend sitting on the edge of the bed, struggling to fasten a clear plastic cup to one of her breasts.

"What's happening?" I asked.

"It's easier this way," she whispered. "The milk isn't always ready to come out, and sometimes when it *is* coming out, she isn't hungry." She managed to secure the cup, and the nipple inside it excreted a yellowish liquid.

I upturned my palms. "No. I mean what the fuck is happening here?"

"Hush!" my girlfriend glared, pointing to a shadowy corner of the bedroom. I peered toward it and discerned a cradle and, inside the cradle, a mound of blankets.

There was a cumulative exasperation boiling up in me—starting with the issues at work and my students' lack of respect and integrity—only to come home to some kind of elaborate prank that, frankly, I found excessive and uninspired. I deliberately raised my voice. "What *is* that thing?"

My girlfriend's face crumpled into a scowl. At the same instant—as if they were the same phenomenon—an abrasive shriek surged from the corner of the bedroom. My girlfriend tore the suction cup from her breast, huffed to the cradle and lifted the knot of blankets into her arms.

"I don't know what you're trying to do," she said, her voice obscured by the shrieking, fluid dripping from her nipple. "But I don't get it and I don't like it and you have no idea how stressful it is here all day alone with her. So if you can't come home and be supportive, then I need you to leave." Her eyes darted away, then back. "I mean the room. I need you to leave the room." She turned her back to me and swayed, coddling the wailing clump of blankets.

I wiped my palms on the front of my pants, as if they were covered in something, and started to speak, to ask reasonably what exactly I had missed. But before I could open my mouth my girlfriend shot a look over her shoulder and jerked her head toward the door. So I went down the hall to my study and sat at my desk, wracking my brain for a memory of the conversation we must have had that would explain what was happening. And I reached the conclusion— which was so obvious—that it was my girlfriend who was misremembering, that she *thought* we'd had a conversation about whatever would explain this, when in fact no such conversation had occurred. Which was why she was acting like *I* was the one who had lost his mind. It was all a misunderstanding, and later, once she'd calmed down, I could explain this to her and we could laugh about it and move on from it, and everything would return to normal.

I set about drafting an e-mail to the dean, who had requested that I relay my understanding of the events surrounding the plagiarism allegation in clear terms and from the beginning. There had been problems since the start of the semester, when I collected the first written assignments from my class and was dismayed at the profusion of unfortunate writing. But one student's writing was particularly poor. At the time I felt bad for him because it was not his failing, but a failing of the system in which he'd grown up. It was a matter of his elementary and high school teachers herding him through, likely at the behest of the education board who were required to show a certain rate of progress in order to get funding, and therefore ignored the glaring learning issues some of their students exhibited. In the case of this one student, they had kicked him down the road from one negligent teacher to the next, onward and upward until he ended up in my English 101 class, which was a writing and research class operating on the assumption that its students possessed at least a passable grasp of grammar mechanics and organizational skills—or at the very least knew how to spell. But the student in this case had none of that knowledge. He had fallen through the cracks, and now that he was in college—a community college with severely limited resources—he was going to struggle to get the basic help he needed in order to improve. With all this in mind, I gave him a C- on his first paper, and advised him to schedule a meeting with me to go over it, after which I would give him an opportunity to resubmit for a higher grade. But he never took advantage of the offer, and the next written assignment—which he submitted a week late —was even worse than the first. Again, I took pity and I gave him another C-, and *again* I offered him the opportunity to meet and discuss ways of raising his grades. And again, he ignored my offer. On top of this he started missing class and failed to submit a couple largish assignments.

Then this last week, when school reconvened after winter break and the students' penultimate research assignments were due, he showed up to class with this keen, beautifully crafted eight-page research paper on satire and irony in Jonathan Swift's "A Modest Proposal" which drew on various credible sources, was expertly cited and arranged, and contained not a single grammatical error or typo. I only needed to read a sentence before concluding he had not written it. I ran it through the school's plagiarism-checker and it came back clean, meaning only that it did not match any previously published material. This meant that someone else had written it for him—probably at a steep price—and I put a giant red F on the first page and returned it to him. It was at that point, as I watched his face contort at the sight of the F, that I decided I should have informed the dean about the plagiarism beforehand, and I made a mental note then and there to send an e-mail after class. But the student got to the dean first and accused me of wrongdoing, of abusing my power, and even apparently of racial bias, as if I had given the F because he was Black, which was particularly mortifying and highly preposterous. But as a result the incident became flipped around, and this student —who had committed the cardinal sin of academia— was calling the shots and rallying support, and *I* was being called to defend myself against charges of misconduct.

It broke my heart that the school, my employer, was willing to humor this charade at the expense of the reputation of one of their professors. I had been nothing but a humble steward to the best interests of my students, and that one entitled, plagiarizing student could come along and jeopardize my commitment was truly dismaying and nearly too much to bear. Frankly, I was considering resigning and seeking employment at an institution that would defend its personnel in the face of injustices like these. I asserted as much in my e-mail to the dean and was about to send it when I heard the door to my study creak behind me.

It was ajar, and darkness boiled in from the hall. I started to get up to close it, assuming a draft had coaxed it open, when a white thing scuttled from the dark into my study. Its face was a cluster of holes. I recoiled, and a gagging noise bubbled up from my throat. I groped out for something—for a weapon—with which to defend myself. My hand found something hard, and I lifted it up, prepared to bludgeon the thing, which advanced on me with startling speed, the holes in its face dilating, contracting, its white body writhing. The thing reared up on its hind legs to attack me, and I started to bring down my arm to strike it, but my girlfriend appeared in the doorway, smiling, and put her hands on her hips.

"Look who found Daddy," she said.

I stood there wedged against the edge of the desk, my breath caught in my throat, eyes darting between my girlfriend—a suction cup dangling from each of her breasts—and the thing on the floor. It stopped a few feet from me, teetered, and fell onto its side. Its stout limbs pawed the air while it whined. My girlfriend sucked her teeth and hurried to it, lifted it into her arms. Outside, a siren screamed down the street, red and blue strobe lights perforating the blinds briefly, and then faded away.

"She's gotten so mobile," my girlfriend said. "I just looked away for a second, and when I looked up she was gone. I didn't realize she could crawl so far. It's all going so fast." She kissed my cheek and lifted the thing—the naked infant—toward me. I fought an impulse to wince at the sight; I looked at my girlfriend and realized she expected me to kiss it. A spate of thoughts and questions bled from my mind and down my spine. I flexed my lips and daubed them against the infant's head—as far from its holes as possible. It smelled like iron and soil. My girlfriend winked and carried the infant from the study, leaving the door open. I managed to take a full breath and looked down at my hand, which was clutching the urn in which my dog's cremated remains were interred. I set it back on the desk carefully and paced around the study for a few minutes, breathing in through my nose and out through my mouth before returning to my desk and discarding the draft of my e-mail to the dean. I started a new e-mail—a less impassioned one—since I decided it might work in my favor, in the long run, if I conveyed just a bit of uncertainty. Though ultimately, really, it was impossible that I was wrong.

An hour later, having sent what in retrospect read as a somewhat sheepish and apologetic e-mail to the dean and spending some time grading journal assignments for my English 99 class, I turned off the lights in my study and felt my way down the hall to the bedroom. My girlfriend breathed steadily in the dark as I undressed and climbed into bed beside her. I started dozing at once and rolled onto my side, the way I always do when I'm falling asleep. Then I remembered the cradle in the corner of the room, and was suddenly wide awake, clutching the sheets, my eyes pared against the pitch-black room. Occasionally, a raspy noise like a chirp or oink would riffle from the dark, and my girlfriend muttered into her pillow a string of ligneous words I could not discern. The radiator gurgled from beside the bed. I resolved that first thing in the morning I would sit down with her and express to her sternly and calmly that I was confused, that I had missed something. Or if this *was* actually a joke or a prank at my expense, that I didn't get it, and I didn't like it, because I was stressed enough with stuff at work, and this was far from helpful. And if it went on much longer it would start to impact my teaching, which would in turn affect my salary. Finally, after some immeasurable period, I drifted off, rehearsing what I would say in the morning. I would start with an assertion, in no uncertain terms, that I loved her, and we just had to get on the same page, and that we could find a way.

When I woke up, my girlfriend was gone and the cradle was empty.

I found her in the kitchen. "Good morning," she said cheerily, spooning yellow pap into a hole in the baby's face. The baby was secured in a highchair at the head of the table, its stubby white hands flat on the tray. From the two holes at the top of its head a pair of glassy eyes wobbled. I sidled to the counter, poured a cup of lukewarm coffee, and sat beside my girlfriend. I watched her profile for some indication of an answer to the questions that had percolated as I slept. She hummed delicately under her breath as she guided the spoon into the baby's biggest hole.

I placed my hand on hers. "We need to talk. I think I missed something—and it's probably my fault. I've been distracted. But I feel like I don't know what's going on here. I don't know how *this* happened," I indicated the baby, "and I need you to explain it to me. Please."

My girlfriend smiled without parting her lips. "I feel that way too sometimes," she said. "Everything moves so fast, it's hard to keep track. And sometimes yeah, I'll look up and ask: 'How did we get here?

What did we miss? Where did all the time go?'" She lifted my hand to her lips and kissed it, set it down on the table, and resumed humming and feeding the baby.

I swallowed a knot of frustration. "You aren't understanding. I mean specifically," I gestured at the highchair, "this *baby*. Where did this *baby* come from? Whose is it…And what's *wrong* with it?" I felt a wave of relief at having managed to articulate the question but my girlfriend was looking at me with her eyes bent and her mouth curled, and I realized I'd scared her. "I mean who am *I*?" I stammered. "Who are *we*? Where did any of us come from? And what's wrong with *all* of us?"

This made her giggle, and she petted my forearm. "I just don't know, my love," she said. "Listen, I'll do everything I can to tire Lamella out today, so she falls asleep early. Then tonight we can watch a movie and just relax. I'll give you a back rub."

An additional set of questions arose, but none felt sufficient to address the extent of my confusion, so instead I merely forced a smile at my girlfriend, and another at the highchair, and then went upstairs and got ready for work.

I forewent shaving for the second day in a row and got in the car about fifteen minutes later than I typically liked. Halfway to campus I realized I'd left the house without saying goodbye to my girlfriend, which was something I'd done in the past that she'd confessed had hurt her feelings, so I called her from the car to apologize, to tell her I loved her and wish her a good day, but she didn't answer. I arrived at campus ten minutes before my first class and hurried from the tier 2 faculty parking lot—about a quarter mile from the building in which I taught—bypassing the café for my usual cup of coffee, and made it to the classroom after most of my students were already seated. I glanced at the syllabus—which, as an adjunct and having had limited involvement compiling, I felt no real affection for—and then started class by asking someone to give me a synopsis of the week's reading, "The Lottery" by Shirley Jackson. No one raised a hand and a few students exchanged looks. I suspected that no one had done the reading and prepared myself for one of *those* classes.

I pointed at a girl in the second row with a dozen piercings in her face. "Michelle," I said. "What can you tell us about 'The Lottery'? What is it about?"

"It's Michaela," she said. "And I think I might have done the wrong reading..." A chorus of students agreed that they, too, had done the wrong reading. I asked them what they had read instead, and they all said, more or less in unison, "Shakespeare's sonnets."

At this point I realized I was teaching the wrong class. This was English 99, and I was teaching English 101. I rubbed my unshaven face and apologized, offering some excuse about how stuff was hectic at home, and fished the correct syllabus out of my bag. We proceeded to have a decent conversation about simile and hyperbole, though I noticed that some of my students were looking at me strangely, studying me, and I feared there might be something on my face, or that my fly was down. When class ended and everyone filed out, I took one of them aside. "Stephen," I said. "Is everything okay?"

"Yeah, everything's good, Professor," he said, and walked away.

An e-mail had come in from the dean during class; she asked that I visit her office at 11:30am to talk. I killed twenty minutes by crossing campus to the café to get a sorely needed coffee. Then I headed up the hill to the administration building, an old stone mansion—conspicuous among the beige, pseudo-modern classroom buildings—that overlooked the campus. I entered through the heavy oak doors, was blasted with dry heat from the overhead vents, and immediately started sweating beneath my scarf. I announced myself to the desk person, an old woman with a square jaw and short-cropped gray hair. She told me to take a seat, and that Dean Oresco would be out shortly. I texted my girlfriend while I waited, asking her how everything was going at home. She responded instantly with a smiley-face emoji and a gun emoji. I texted back, 'Ditto,' and then, worried that she might think I was comparing my problems with hers, I followed it up with, 'But I can't imagine...' before sliding the phone back into my pocket and wiping my damp palms across my lap.

At about 11:39 a pair of young men about my age —each in a suit worth three months of my salary— exited the dean's office, laughing. Dean Oresco's head emerged behind them and she motioned to me. "Come in, Mel," she said.

I had never been in her office before and was struck by the jarring discrepancy between its luxuriant décor and the utilitarian style of the rest of the campus. Dean Oresco indicated a chair by her desk and sat across from me. She leaned back, cleared her throat, and seemed either to smile or grimace. "How are things?" she asked.

"Fine," I said. "Everything's fine."

Her eyes narrowed and she nodded slowly, as if I had just offered a great deal of information that required careful parsing. "How are your classes?"

"For the most part they're good," I said. "I have some very bright students this year..." A handful of seconds passed in silence. "And for the most part I'm just happy to see how invested most of them are in learning. That's more important than their grades, I think."

Dean Oresco's expression held. "Of course," she said. "You know, this is the first real education a lot of our students are receiving. Especially our immigrant students. For them this is a tremendous, once-in-a-lifetime opportunity."

I nodded. I wasn't sure what she wanted me to say. There was a set of white bookends, each in the shape of a girl's profile, looking off in opposite directions on the windowsill behind her. There were no books between them. The window overlooked the campus's main lawn, broken out in sallow patches of snow. Beyond it the sky was pale.

"I assume you received the e-mail," I said. "That you requested."

"We're just waiting for Samanta," Dean Oresco said. "I want to have her here for that conversation."

I tilted my head.

"My assistant," she said. "It's just nice to have someone else in the room."

"Of course." I uncoiled my scarf from my neck and set it on my lap and attempted, as subtly as possible, to wipe sweat from my upper lip with the back of my hand.

"How's your family?" Dean Oresco asked.

"My girlfriend is fine, busy." A rush of thoughts like a swarm of birds beat around my head. I shrugged. "Everybody's fine."

"Good. That's good," Dean Oresco leaned back and crossed her legs.

We sat, looking past one another, for nearly a full minute. Then a door at the side of the room opened, and a slender young woman with wet, dark eyes entered. "I'm so sorry," she said, somewhat out of breath. "I got stuck with Victor discussing these stupid TEAS exams." She stopped at the side of the desk and pushed her dark hair away from her narrow face.

"Sit here next to me," Dean Oresco motioned to a chair beside her that I hadn't noticed. "Samanta, this is Mel Lane, he's one of our adjuncts. Mel, this is Samanta Sewenger, my assistant."

Samanta, already half-seated, stood back up and leaned across the desk with her hand extended. "Nice to meet you," she said.

"Likewise," I said. Her hand was dry, and I worried she registered the perspiration on my palm. I reminded myself that I no longer cared about how the condition of my body was perceived by other women, because I was in love with my girlfriend.

Dean Oresco folded her hands on the desk. I looked back and forth between her and Samanta. Samanta's mouth curled up at the edges each time my eyes landed on her, and then immediately collapsed when I looked away, as if smiling caused her great discomfort.

"Alright," Dean Oresco said. "Obviously you know why we're here, Mel. We want to get this thing sorted out as quickly as possible. Now I've read your e-mail, and I've spoken with the administrators who you met with yesterday, and I think I understand your side of all this. But I want to make sure we're all on the same page. Is that alright?"

"Of course," I crossed my legs.

"Good. Okay. So according to your e-mail, this student, Carl Jones, had been performing poorly in your class for most of the semester, correct?"

"Yes. Quite poorly."

"And so in what ways exactly was his performance poor?"

I cleared my throat. "His writing, mostly, was…it was just bad. Just a very menial grasp of basic grammatical stuff, tons of spelling errors, no real understanding of the material. Kind of a combination of ignorance and laziness."

Samanta's eyes flashed, for a second, to Dean Oresco.

"I mean, it's not his fault, of course," I continued, uncrossing my legs. "I recognize that he was just coming in with, you know, a lifetime of being neglected by his educators. I certainly don't blame him for that. And I went out of my way to give him the opportunity to meet with me, one-on-one, to talk about this stuff and try to get his writing into a better place."

"Did he ever meet with you?"

"He never took me up on the offer. He submitted two papers in the first half of the semester, both of which received C minuses, and on both of which I clearly noted that I would be happy to meet with him during office hours."

"Did you ever approach him in person, before or after class maybe, to offer further help?"

"Well, no. But the thing is, after I returned that second paper, he kind of stopped showing up. I mean he was there occasionally, but he missed at least two classes. Two or three."

"So he wasn't engaged."

"Correct."

"I see," Dean Oresco made some gesture to Samanta, who wrote something down on a yellow legal pad. "So then what happened?"

"It's all in my e-mail," I said. "We reconvened after winter break, and he turned in his third assignment. I could tell within the first page—less— that something was wrong."

"Wrong?"

"That he hadn't written it."

"He claims very adamantly that he did."

"He's lying."

"Is it possible—just possible—that he may have decided to apply himself on this assignment? That what we're seeing here is the best work he can do versus the work he produces with minimal effort?"

I shook my head and shrugged. "I mean, there's a possibility of anything, sure."

Samanta wrote something on the legal pad. Dean Oresco took a breath and leaned back. "The problem is, Mel, that an accusation of plagiarism is taken very seriously on *both* sides. It's grounds for expulsion on the side of the student, if it's proven, but it's also grounds for...certain measures...on the side of the faculty accuser, if it proves unfounded."

I wiped my palms on my lap. "So for the future," I said, "how do you suggest I proceed, if something like this happens again?"

"Let's take one thing at a time," Dean Oresco said. "We're looking at the paper in question, as well as the previous papers for contrast. If we can determine that in fact Carl Jones plagiarized his paper, then we will take the proper disciplinary steps. Though—and I must say this—you still really did not handle this situation correctly, if I'm being frank."

"Well that's why I asked, you know, for the future..."

"And you should be aware that if we find no evidence of plagiarism, then we're going to have to take that very seriously as well."

"I understand that." I looked at the windowpane behind the two women. "For the record," I said. "I realize now I mishandled this. I thought I was doing the right thing."

"No one ever means to do the wrong thing," Samanta Sewenger said, and Dean Oresco and I both looked at her. She reddened as she continued. "I mean, even people who commit really heinous crimes think they're doing the right thing, to some extent..."

Dean Oresco shrugged her eyebrows. "Anyway," she said. "It's just important that you understand this is ongoing. Carl Jones is threatening to turn this into a big thing, accusing you and the school of all kinds of biases—which for the record I don't think are founded—but we have to take those seriously as well."

"Of course."

"Do you have any questions for me?"

"No. Not at the moment. I would just...I like working here, and I really care about my students. And I never meant for any of this to become..."

Dean Oresco stood, and Samanta stood, and I stood. "We'll keep you informed about how it all plays out," Dean Oresco said. "Meanwhile, we've transferred your English 101 course over to Robin Cliff. Just for the time being, until we can determine how to proceed."

"You mean I'm not teaching my class anymore?"

"Not English 101. You're fine to continue with your other classes. But we want to keep you and Carl Jones apart for now, until we have a conclusion on our end." Dean Oresco folded her hands at her waist and I nodded at Samanta, whose mouth curled at the edges. I stood for a few seconds longer than I should have, and then turned and left the office.

Without my English 101 class, I had no reason to stay on campus. On the way to my car, I received a text from my girlfriend asking that I pick up a few things from the supermarket after work. It wasn't even noon, and I considered doing something with my day. But every option I considered—going to the movies, taking myself shopping, strolling through a museum—struck me as lonely and laborious, and eventually I resigned to do nothing. I texted my girlfriend that I would be home early, with groceries.

As I drove, I listened to the radio at a low volume; the voices were muffled as if having a conversation in another room that did not concern me. I was not used to making the drive home from campus at any time of day other than morning and evening rush hour, and the ease with which I proceeded north was unsettling. I had the strangest sensation that I was missing some vital information, information that would have complicated the commute, but was also necessary in order to complete it at all.

In the checkout line at the supermarket, I watched the woman ahead of me unload a bulging cartful of mostly frozen meals and cases of soda onto the counter. She seemed frazzled by the sheer quantity of her items. Her daughter, maybe five or six years old, stood off to the side, thumbing through the candy rack, occasionally taking a chocolate bar or a bag of gummies and placing it casually onto the counter. The woman would snatch up the candy and replace it on the shelf, and then fix her daughter with a glare. At one point the woman turned to me and rolled her eyes. "What are you gonna do?" she said.

I shrugged.

"Do you have kids?" she asked me.

"No," I said, unloading my items onto the counter behind hers.

"Smart man," she said, then stage-whispered: "They suck the life out of you."

"So I've heard," I said, placing my empty basket below the counter. Then I added, "There are too many things I want to do."

"Well, good for you. Get it while you can. The time just slips away." She paid for her groceries, loaded the dozen or so bags into her cart, and walked off. Her daughter gamboled along behind her.

In the car I checked my phone and found a voicemail from my mom.

"Hi sweetie. Thinking about you guys. The biggest thing for me at first was getting enough sleep. Sleep in shifts! And let me know if there's anything I can do to help out. Love you."

I tossed the phone onto the passenger seat and drove off. I experienced a rambling series of thoughts that refused cohesion, like too many people talking at once. I tried to decipher what my mom had meant by "The biggest thing *for me...*" —as if she had been through something *I* was currently going through— and I was, again, wracking my brain for the conversation that must have transpired between me and my girlfriend, the conversation that would explain everything. Because there was a perfectly reasonable explanation, one that everyone around me seemed to be aware of and yet eluded me entirely. I was so distracted by all this that I blew halfway through a stop sign, causing an oncoming car to scream to a halt and blare its horn at me. I waved, embarrassed, but was already too far into the intersection to let the car pass. So I continued on and tried to breathe and steady my thoughts and remind myself that all that was needed was a reasonable and honest conversation with my girlfriend.

Back home, I did not immediately go inside. I let the car idle in the driveway, feeling suddenly and utterly exhausted. I checked my e-mail, but there was nothing. I considered writing to Dean Oresco, to follow up on some points I'd made earlier, or to clarify my argument, or profess an apology. Instead, I slid my phone into my pocket, gathered up the grocery bags, and hauled myself from the car.

As I stepped inside, something scurried past my legs and disappeared around the corner. I froze, clutching the bags. My girlfriend appeared at the foot of the stairs. She was flushed, and her hair was matted in oily strands around the frame of her face. "Hi!" she said, grinning. "We're playing tag. I think you're it."

The patter of bare feet on wooden floor issued from elsewhere in the house. The television was on in the den, cartoonish voices guffawing from it. I held out the bags to my girlfriend. "I think I need to lie down for a bit," I said, attempting to sound as tired as possible.

My girlfriend took the bags and frowned. "You look beat up, love," she said. She wore a tank top, and her exposed arms, with the grocery bags dangling from them, were sinewy and lean. She had always been rounded, tender, and I could not remember when that had changed.

I shut myself in the bedroom. I lay down on top of the blankets, having bothered only to remove my shoes, and I stared up at the ceiling. For the first time I noticed a narrow crack in the paint like a vein from the molding on one side to the ceiling's center. Had it just appeared today? I rolled onto my side because looking at the crack made me nauseous, and I realized I hadn't put anything in my stomach all day except coffee. It was a terrible habit I'd had since adolescence, one I always swore I would break. I considered getting up for a glass of water to settle my stomach, but in that moment I was smothered by sleepiness, and drifted off into shallow, slithering dreams.

My girlfriend and my mom and Carl Jones, all engaged in hushed conversation at the far end of a wide room in which I was alone against the opposite wall. I approached them, to confront them about their scheming. As I approached, Carl Jones raised a hand at me and shook his head, to which my girlfriend nodded in agreement. Except she didn't look like my girlfriend, but rather like Samanta Sewenger. One by one they walked off, until I was left alone with my mom, who looked like Dean Oresco, and she put her hand on my shoulder gravely, and then walked off to join the others, who were speaking again, quietly, away from me in this wide, white room. And here it occurred to me that the room itself was moving, scurrying around inside an even *larger* room, with me sealed inside, and I awoke slowly, jostled by the room's jerky movements. The bedroom was dark, and a shrill scream rattled through the house.

I turned on lights as I went downstairs. My girlfriend was in the den, sitting on the edge of the sofa with her face in her hands. In the middle of the floor sat a pale, naked toddler. The holes in its face contorted into various shapes of distress as it screamed a corroding note. I stopped in the doorway. My girlfriend looked up at me and gestured to the toddler. "She needs her daddy," she said. The toddler groped with its knobby hands. Its wail pitched up an octave.

I stepped toward it, then paused. "What do I do?" I asked.

"*Hold* her!" my girlfriend shot her arms out as if to strike something. The toddler clawed the air. I went to it, squatted beside it, and slid my hands beneath its arms. It lurched toward me, grasping at my collar. I lifted it, suppressing my aversion, and embraced it. At once, as if someone had flipped a switch, the crying ceased. The toddler nestled its open face into my neck. I smelled the ferric, earthy odor of it, its skin dry like paper. It cooed hoarsely in my ear, its breathing slow, seeming to grow heavier in my arms.

My girlfriend stroked the toddler's white skull. She kissed my cheek and led me upstairs. I started toward the bedroom but she stopped me. "Where are you going?" she whispered.

"To the crib," I whispered back.

"No, stupid." She opened the door to my study and turned on the light. My books were gone, as was my desk and my reading chair and the artwork I'd hung on the walls. Now there was a small, white dresser, and a changing table in one corner. Against the far wall, a low bed with white sheets. I stood in the doorway with the toddler's weight. My girlfriend folded back the sheets on the bed and straightened the pillow. "Put her down," she said. "Gentle."

The floor creaked as I crossed the room. I lowered the toddler onto the bed. Its little hands clasped my collar, and I unfastened them carefully. My girlfriend pulled the sheets up around its shoulders and tucked them in around the edges of its small body. We stood there and looked down at it—its holey, white head, its weight compressing the white pillow, the contours of its bent legs beneath the white sheets. I noticed clusters of white flakes clinging to my shirt, like dandruff, and brushed at them.

"Her skin's dry," my girlfriend said. "It's normal. It'll stop soon."

She led me from the room, closing the door softly, and down the hall. We sat on our bed together and she put her head in my lap, and I stroked her hair away from her face. "I'm so happy it's the weekend," I said, yawning.

"Love," my girlfriend ran her hand along my thigh. "It's Thursday."

I laughed, charmed as usual by her dry humor. But she was not smiling, and I counted back through the week on my fingers. "My god..." I said. "How did I lose track of time like that?"

"There's been a lot going on," my girlfriend traced a shape on my knee. "It's not unusual, in situations like this, to get a little turned around."

"Situations like this..." I echoed, playing back the last few days in my head, step by step, trying to account for every bit of time. I remembered grading papers last night and writing the e-mail to Dean Oresco... "Wait," I said, jolted suddenly alert. "Where are Olive's ashes?"

"What?"

"Olive's ashes. They were on my desk last night, where they always are. Where did you move them?"

"I didn't touch them, love," my girlfriend said. "Remember? You told me not to, that you would put them somewhere safe."

I shut my eyes. "Did I?"

"It's okay. They're with your books, I think."

"My books…"

She pushed me onto my back. "We're both so stressed," she said, straddling my waist. "Let's help each other unwind."

She removed her tank top and unclasped her bra. Her breasts looked different, I thought, than they usually did. They were lined with blue veins, and the skin between them clung to her sternum. Her nipples were wider and darker than I remembered. She leaned forward and kissed my mouth, her breath sour and her lips cracked and coppery. She kissed my neck, my chest, and I laced my fingers behind my head and gazed at the ceiling, where the crack ran across.

"We gotta get someone in to fix this ceiling," I said. My girlfriend mumbled something in reply. I sighed and closed my eyes. I thought about my meeting with Dean Oresco, tried to replay our conversation word-for-word, looking for places where I could have represented myself better, or stood up for myself more. I tried to imagine what she and her assistant, Samanta, might have talked about after I'd left. Had Samanta defended me? Or did she—like everyone else seemed to—suspect me of impropriety?

I wondered what Samanta thought about Dean Oresco in general. Did she admire her? Revere her? Was she indifferent? I imagined Samanta and I talking over coffee in the campus café, laughing about Dean Oresco's baroque office, or about Carl Jones's horrible early-semester essays. Each time I made a joke her mouth curled up at the edges—moved to smile despite it being painful for her—and her dark hair slid out from behind her ear, and she tucked it back with a thin hand. She was shy, and sweet, and her lips were much fuller than her narrow face. I imagined her setting down her coffee, glancing coyly around the café, sliding down onto the floor, crawling beneath the table toward me, looking up at me with her big, wet eyes while unbuckling my pants, stroking me, licking me right there in the middle of the café while students mulled about eating lunch and doing homework. Her mouth was wet, and it curled up at the edges, and I reached down and tucked her dark hair behind her ear, and her cheeks reddened. She stopped for a second, to say something profound: "Everyone always *thinks* they're doing the right thing," and then started again. I flexed and groaned, kneaded her hair. And we were no longer in the café, but in my bed, and she was tugging off her pants and clambering up until she was straddling my face, and I lapped and kissed her...But she didn't taste like I thought she would—which was of cinnamon or musky flowers—but instead she tasted sour, and coppery. She tasted familiar. When I looked up she was not Samanta, but my girlfriend with her back arched, grinding her hips on my chin. I held her thighs, to guide her to slow down. But she went faster, a low, phlegmy sound rising from her throat. Something thick and hot and metallic leaked into my mouth, and I tried to push her off me but she resisted. I pushed harder, managing to displace her, and she flopped onto her back and scowled at me. But then her face softened—she wiped at my lips and her fingers came back red, and she wiped between her legs and then held up both hands.

"I'm so sorry..." she said. "Oh my god." She hurried down the hall, returning with a wad of toilet paper in one hand and a tampon in the other. And after we'd cleaned ourselves up, she sat down next to me and took my hand. "I'm really so sorry," she said. "That's awful. I had no idea that was going to happen."

"It's okay," I said. "I gotta say that's a first for me. I'm glad it was with you."

She put her face in her hands. When she looked up, she was smiling. "Well, that wasn't exactly what I had in mind." She pointed at my lap. "Do you want me to finish?"

I shrugged. "I think I'm fine for now. Thanks."

"You must be hungry," she said. "Let's eat something."

We went downstairs and rummaged around the kitchen until we'd managed to scrounge up a meal from a smattering of leftovers. We sat on the sofa in the den in front of the television while we ate. Years ago, when we first moved in together—when I was still in grad school and she was still working at various bars and restaurants around town—we would convene in the den late every night, just like this, and eat on the sofa while watching television. More often than not we would fall asleep here, wake up before sunrise and one of us would carry the other upstairs to the bed for another hour or two of sleep. I always used to be the first out of bed and would return downstairs, clear the previous night's dishes from the coffee table, and make a pot of coffee. Back then I still thought I could be a novelist. I would take my coffee up to the study and write for an hour or two until my girlfriend woke up. But then I graduated, and I couldn't sell my book, and she quit her jobs at the restaurants and bars because the lifestyle was giving her anxiety attacks. Soon after, I got my adjunct position at the college, which was about all my MFA qualified me to do. I started having to grade papers at night, and her workless schedule allowed her to eat early, which she preferred, and our nightly dinners in the den together evaporated. In general, over the last couple years we saw less and less of one another. I hadn't realized how much I missed that time—sitting next to her, watching television, not even talking but just being near—until that moment. It felt so nice. But it also felt too late. This was an imitation of the original, a going-through-the-motions for old-time's sake. We would never have that back, though if I pushed these thoughts aside, stared at the television, and moved my knee just a few inches so it pressed against hers, it almost felt, just for a moment, like the real thing.

A white shape stole through the hall and stopped just outside the room. I dropped my fork, startled, as a knot of holes peered around the doorframe and into the den.

"Lamella, what are you doing up?" My girlfriend crossed the room and squatted in front of the naked child, who stepped shyly into the light. Tufts of white hair sprouted from its skull.

"I had a nightmare," it croaked, and I was appalled by its voice.

"Poor baby," my girlfriend stroked its head. "Let me put you back in bed."

"I want Daddy," it said, and looked at me with its glassy eyes through the holes in its face.

I looked down at my food, my eyes probing as if searching for something hiding inside it.

My girlfriend kissed the child on its head. "Daddy will take you back to bed while I put away these dishes, okay?"

"Can I sleep with you?" it rasped.

"You're too old for that now," said my girlfriend. "But I know Daddy will stay with you until you fall asleep." She gathered up the plates and disappeared into the kitchen, leaving me alone with the child, who eyed me expectantly.

"Come on, Daddy," it said, taking my hand and tugging me to the stairs.

In the dark, with only pale light from the downstairs hallway bleeding in, the study looked encrusted in snow. The child led me to its bed, climbed onto it, and sat with the soles of its feet pressed together. It looked at me, and I counted the holes in its face—there was an even number—and I counted again—and the number was odd—and its naked skin, in the vague light, was the same color as the room.

I arranged the blankets over its body, tucking them in around its shoulders the way my girlfriend had earlier. It looked up at me, and I felt like I should say something but could think of nothing that would not give away my disconcertion—both to the child and to myself. I sat on the edge of the bed with my hands in my lap, gazing toward the door through which faint light bubbled in. I felt the child's eyes on me and smelled the metallic, wet-earthiness of it. I wanted to hide my face.

I looked down, and the holes around the child's eyes were gawping at me as if in terror. I stood abruptly and retreated from the bed. The eyes followed me across the room, huge and pared. "Stop," I tried to say, though nothing came out but a line of air. I tried again, and this time the word emerged but raspy, like the child's voice, and I realized that it was *not* me who had spoken, but that it was the child, repeating, "Stop, stop," as if *I* was the one frightening *it*. I felt along the wall for the doorway—but there was nothing but more wall. The child's eyes bored into me. I wanted to scream. I wanted to sink into myself.

Something rose up beside me, and I recoiled—but it was my girlfriend, holding a glass of water. "Is she asleep?" she whispered.

Across the room, there was nothing but a tangle of sheets, and a lump beneath it. I stammered a sentence of breathy gibberish and clasped my girlfriend's shoulder.

"My god," she said. "You're shaking."

I tried to take a slow breath. My girlfriend started toward the bed, and I reached out for her to stop, to tell her not to. But by the time I could muster the air and the energy to speak, she had already set down the glass of water on the nightstand and was by my side once more; she put her hand on my arm, and we left the room.

In the bedroom we undressed and got into bed. "Did you have another panic attack?" she asked. This was a strange question, because *she* was the one who used to suffer panic attacks, not me. But then I remembered—how could I have forgotten?—that some years ago, when I started teaching at the college, I came home one evening and, while standing in the den with my coat still on and my bag hanging from my shoulder, I felt my breath catch suddenly, my vision tapered, and I was overwhelmed by the conviction that I was about to die. I sat down on the floor, which is where my girlfriend found me, and I told her I was having a heart attack, about which she was skeptical, but agreed to drive me to the hospital.

There I was told that my heart was fine, and everything else checked out physiologically, and it was likely anxiety that had caused the attack. This was a relief, but also somewhat more disturbing—that such a powerful, visceral sensation could be triggered by my own mind. I was prescribed a medication to take in the future at the onset of another such attack, though I had never needed it.

"No, this wasn't a panic attack," I said beside her in bed.

My girlfriend stroked my forehead. "Then what happened?"

I sighed three times. "I don't know," I said. "Maybe it *was* a panic attack."

My girlfriend kissed my nose. "Everything's okay," she said. "I promise that everything is okay…" She got up and left the room and returned with a glass of water, which she set on the nightstand beside me. She got into bed and shut off the lights, and the blue glow of her phone seemed to cast years of age across her face, so she looked like her mother.

I slept fitfully, startled repeatedly awake from the cusp of sleep by sounds in the house. As morning approached, I found myself staring up at the crack in the dark ceiling, the sheets knotted around me, mesmerized by the snaps and gurgles of the radiator.

At around a quarter to five I got up, dressed, and crept downstairs. I gathered my work stuff, which I'd left scattered around the den, got in the car and drove through the dark in the general direction of campus. I had three hours before I had to be at work for a faculty meeting, and then, without my English 101 class, I had nothing until late in the afternoon.

I drove south on local roads that braced the river, parallel to the train tracks, past a row of warehouses that sprawled off into the dark, and past the nuclear power plant that loomed over the water, bleeding palls of gray smoke up into the puckering sky. I took a road that led off for half a mile through a city of storage units until it petered out into a dead end, then backtracked and continued south through residential neighborhoods, where occasionally I would slow as trucks backed out of driveways in front of me, and the men inside showed me their palms and then rumbled off down the street, belching clouds of exhaust. I passed shopping centers of pizzerias and liquor stores and laundromats, all dark and indifferent. I pulled into a Gulf station to put gas in the car. It was cold out, and my fingers burned as I squeezed the pump, and my breath billowed around me in gray plumes. I went inside for a cup of coffee, waiting in line behind a group of men—who chatted with each other and with the cashier in Spanish and paid for their coffees with cash and coins—and when I got to the counter, I used my debit card to pay the $2.25 and the machine took a long time to process. As I waited, the door chimed and a pair of teenagers walked in, a boy and a girl. They looked strung-out and squirrely, and I instinctively watched them from the corner of my eye as they flitted around the store. I peered through the glass doors out into the pinkening morning at my car, to make sure it wasn't being robbed. Eventually the machine beeped, and I removed my card and took my coffee, got back in my car and drove on.

On the highway, I noticed the radio was on at a faint volume, voices chattering about things I could not discern. I considered turning it up, or turning it off completely, but something about the lack of clarity felt important, as if it were a code that was only decipherable in its obscurity. If I turned it up, and heard it clearly, then the code would devolve into banality. If I turned it off, I would lose the opportunity to learn it at all. And so I drove with the voices speaking lowly, the beginnings and ends of the words swallowed up in an abstruse pattern of consonants. After a while it started to feel as though something was coming through, like maybe I was starting to understand, though I couldn't describe *what* I was understanding other than that I was learning something, a secret truth, palpable and significant, and I strained to hear it—not the words but the caps and fractures of the words, because only in that breakdown was there something real, something honest, and before I knew it I was pulling onto campus, two hours early. I parked in the tier 2 faculty lot, sat back, sipped my coffee, and gazed through the windshield at a patchy copse of trees strewn with garbage that seemed to darken as the sky filled with light.

I opened my eyes, and the light was different. I blinked as I looked blearily around the car. The clock on the dash showed 8:15. I pulled out my phone, which was in agreement, and I huffed and clambered from the car. Halfway across the parking lot I realized I'd left my bag—and had left the car running—and I ran back, grabbed my bag from the backseat and shut off the engine, then hurried across campus toward the Academic Center, to a faculty meeting to which I was all of a sudden late.

Students trudged around under the weights of their backpacks. A maintenance truck hunkered down a walking path, its tires carving ruts in the frosted grass to either side. I made it to the Academic Center only somewhat out of breath and jogged down the hall to the conference room. But the room was empty. I returned to the entrance and asked the desk person where the 8:00am faculty meeting was. He motioned to the same hall down which I had just been, and I started to protest but did not have the energy for a conversation, so went again down the hall. The room was, of course, still empty, and I turned in a circle. Across the hall was another conference room, and through the long windows I saw rows of my colleagues, seated with their backs to me, and a woman at the front of the room gesturing at a slide panel on the wall behind her. I crept inside, distracting only a handful of people in the rows near the door. I sat in the back and tried to take long, measured breaths into my nose and out of my mouth.

After a few minutes I noticed I was sitting directly next to Samanta Sewenger. I crossed my legs. She had her yellow legal pad in her lap, and wore a navy-blue blouse and a long, crimson skirt that ended just above her ankles and her puce boots. In total, her outfit was rich and vital and brought to mind bushels of ripe berries and expensive upholstery. I caught myself staring at her skirt, and when I looked up, she was watching me. My face warmed. The edges of her mouth curled up. I averted my eyes. The woman at the front of the room pointed to a slide of a graph indicating something about student truancy rates—though I could not tell if the graph showed them rising or falling.

When the meeting ended and we all filed out of the room, I found myself walking alongside Samanta. I tried to think of something to say, but it was as if my entire vocabulary had been burglarized, and all I could do was chew the inside of my lip.

Finally, as we neared the building's exit, she spoke. "So how are you feeling about what happened?"

I thought she was referring to the impromptu nap I'd taken in the parking lot—though of course she had no way of knowing about that. "What do you mean?" I asked.

"This plagiarism investigation," she said.

I was surprised at how surprised I was. Somehow I'd managed to go all morning without thinking about it. "'Investigation' makes it sound so serious," I said.

Her mouth curled at the edges. "Well it *is* kind of serious, I guess. But just for the record I saw the paper in question, and the other papers from earlier in the semester, and I think you're right. It really does not seem like they were written by the same person."

A group of faculty members neared, one of them clearing his throat, and we stepped aside to let them pass.

"I appreciate you saying that," I said. "I've been feeling like a crazy person, like I'm seeing reality differently than everyone else."

"I know what you mean," Samanta said. "I feel that way too, sometimes."

"You do?"

"Sure. Sometimes I feel like everybody else knows something I don't, like I didn't get the memo. It's like being somewhere where you don't speak the language, and everyone around you is laughing, or scared, and you have no idea what the joke is. Or the danger."

"Exactly."

"So you're not alone."

"I'm glad to have you for company."

Samanta's mouth curled.

"Do you want to grab a coffee?" I asked. "I don't have to teach until this afternoon."

She looked behind her as if startled by a loud noise as if at a loud noise, then turned back to me and whispered. "Don't you have, like, a wife and a kid?"

I cleared my throat. "I mean, no. I'm not married. Though yeah, I mean, I have a girlfriend. But I just meant, like, as friends, or acquaintances. As in, you know, just a cup of coffee."

Samanta pushed a lock of dark hair behind her ear and shifted her weight away from me. "I actually have to be all the way across campus soon, so…"

"Of course," I said. "It's all good. Maybe another time."

Her mouth curled minutely—though it may have been the light shifting over her face as she walked away—and I was left standing alone against the wall, imagining a giant hole was opening inside my head.

The rest of the day unfolded as a single, leaky moment. When it was over, I made my way back toward my car. It had gotten cold, windy, and overcast—the walkway lamps were on, despite sunset being several hours away. I passed the Student Center, grasping my coat shut at the collar and squinting into the wind, when I saw Carl Jones coming down the path toward me. Three more young men flanked him, and as they noticed me I put my head down and quickened my pace, trying to hurry past.

Carl's voice swirled in the wind beside me. "Professor Lane?"

I stopped and looked up as if noticing him for the first time. I let go of my coat, which blew open and billowed out on either side of me, and I held up my hands. "I don't want any trouble," I said.

Carl blinked at me, and his friends, gathered behind him, blinked too. "I just wanted to apologize," he said. "I didn't mean for all this to become such a big deal. I just, I really *did* write that paper, and I worked really hard on it, and I was just...I thought I deserved better than an F. Because it was better than the other ones, and you gave those C minuses, so... And just...I didn't mean for this to all get so crazy."

I eyed his friends, who stood behind him. One of them, I thought, might have been in my class last year, though I wasn't certain.

Finally, after too many seconds had passed, Carl shrugged and hung his head, and he and his friends walked off. I watched them go. Farther down the path, one of the young men took Carl's hand, and Carl leaned his head on the young man's shoulder. I clutched my coat tightly against the wind and continued to my car. By the time I got there my fingertips were burning with cold, and my nose was running. I turned the heat up all the way and reminded myself that I had not done anything wrong. I was a good teacher and a good boyfriend. There were misunderstandings occasionally. It was no one's fault. And Carl Jones had plagiarized that paper—

there was no question. He was simply trying to cover his tracks.

As I drove, I replayed my conversation with Samanta Sewenger. I was sure that whatever had happened had more to do with her than with me. Her intense reluctance to get coffee—a simple cup of coffee—sprang from something in her life, her own indecisiveness or insecurity. I didn't know anything about her, and anything was possible. Maybe she was one of those people who liked to have control, and when someone else took control she got uncomfortable and scrambled to take it back. She did not exactly strike me as this kind of person—except that probably everyone was, in their own way. This thought reminded me of what she said yesterday, about how no one ever did anything they did not think was right. She really was so clever. I tried to apply her logic to my behavior. How was asking another woman out for coffee the right thing? Or how did I *think* it was the right thing in that moment? No matter how I turned it or bent it or reworded it in my head, I still sounded like a slime-ball, or at the very least an idiot.

As I merged onto the highway, another thought struck me: Would this affect the investigation? Would Samanta report back to Dean Oresco that I had asked her out? Would she embellish it and claim that I said something inappropriate to her, or touched her arm in a threatening manner? Because I didn't know Samanta, or what she might be capable of. And here I had put myself in this situation where plenty of people had seen us together in the hall, and not one of them had witnessed the entire interaction. Not one of them had seen me *not* touch her arm, or *not* make an indecorous advance. Add to this the ongoing investigation and it was possible—given the choices I had made over the last week—that at best my job was in jeopardy, and at worst my career in academia was endangered.

My girlfriend's car was gone, and the house was empty. I called her but she did not answer. I changed into sweatpants and a t-shirt, and set about looking for Olive's urn. I had no memory of moving it. I checked the usual places: windowsills, closet shelves, the deep drawers of the dresser in the bedroom. I went to the basement and prodded among the junk— but I could not imagine myself putting her down here in this dusty, unlit place. The attic, on the other hand, was spacious, and lit by opposing east/west-facing windows, and it gathered little dust, and it was warm. I searched among the rows of unused lamps and plastic bins of old clothes, convinced that she was here, that I was close. I found a cardboard box of books—old textbooks and binders that I'd never bothered to unpack after the move. I found my old printer, the one I had used to print copies of my manuscript to mail to publishers—although they would gladly have accepted it via e-mail, likely preferred it, but I found the printed copy in an envelope to be romantic, and convinced myself that it increased my chances of selling the book. It very well may have had the opposite effect. I found a copy of the manuscript itself, tattered and yellowing, and I thumbed through it, cringing, eventually folding it over and wedging it into the box of textbooks and tossing a rug over it. I sighed and rubbed my face, forgetting for a moment what I was doing in the attic. Only a minute ago I was convinced that Olive was here, and yet now I was certain she was not. I turned in a slow circle, scanning the sprawl of stuff. There was a girl standing at the top of the staircase. I gasped and put my hand on my heart.

Its glassy eyes glistened from the holes in its face. Its head was slightly cocked, and its white hair dangled in clumps to its shoulders. Its naked, prepubescent body was as white as bone. I averted my eyes.

"What are you doing up here?" it wheezed.

As if to prove I was unperturbed by its presence, I crouched and sifted through a box. "I'm looking for something," I said.

"What are you looking for?"

I pretended to look around the attic. "An urn," I said.

"What's that?"

"For ashes. My dog, Olive, is in it." Then I added, "It's very important to me."

"Can I help you look?" the girl's voice was like gravel underfoot.

"It's red, a red box, about this big," I indicated with my hands. The girl started to step into the attic, its wide gaze toppling across the stuff on the floor, and I held up my hand. "But I don't think it's up here," I said. "If you want to help me, check around other parts of the house."

The girl watched as I stooped down and sorted through another box—this one full of my girlfriend's summer clothing. I felt it standing there, just feet from me, and I wanted to throw something at it, or scream for it to get away. I sighed and looked at it, at the holes in its face, the eyes and the nubby teeth, and I wanted to say: "What? What do you want? What are you *doing* here?" But my girlfriend's head appeared at the staircase. Her face was nervous and flushed. The tepid light of the attic revealed stray gray strands in her otherwise dark hair.

"You two need to come help me get ready," she said, pointing at me and the girl.

"Help you get ready for what?" I asked.

"My parents are on their way over, for dinner," she said. "Lamella and I were at the movies when they called and invited themselves. We have to get the place cleaned up and get something in the oven."

"Okay, I'm coming right now," I said.

The girl's eyes tumbled in their holes. Even from feet away I could smell its odor of iron and dirt.

"You too, Lamella," said my girlfriend.

Downstairs, I straightened up the house while my girlfriend toiled in the kitchen. When I went to check on her, she waved me away, busy chopping and stirring and moving something from one oven rack to another. I swept beneath the sofa in the den, wiped down the dining room table, carried a stack of random detritus—a few cups, an old newspaper, a pile of bills—out of sight, and lit some candles along the windowsills.

I went upstairs to change. The door to the study was ajar, and I peered inside. The girl was there, standing at a full-length mirror mounted to the wall, looking at itself. It brushed its hands along its hair, down its chest and thighs, turned and looked at itself over its shoulder, over the other shoulder, turned again and leaned toward the mirror until its face was two inches from the glass, one inch, pressed against it. The glass fogged with its breath, and it drew something in the condensation with its index finger. It shifted its weight, studied itself, and swayed back and forth in a slow, jerky dance. It raised its arms over its head and folded its elbows back and shifted its weight. I looked at the mirror, and the girl's wide eyes were looking back at me. I hurried away down the hall to the bedroom and changed back into my work clothes. When I reemerged into the hall, the door to the study was closed. I padded softly past the door and tiptoed downstairs.

My girlfriend's parents brought a bottle of red wine and a chocolate cake in a red bakery box. "I like the scruffy look," my girlfriend's dad said, slapping me on the back. They busied themselves in the kitchen with my girlfriend, commandeering the preparation. I poured four glasses of wine and handed them around. My girlfriend's dad tended to the chicken in the oven, which he said she was cooking too fast. My girlfriend shrugged and drank her wine and said she hadn't had a choice, since she hadn't known they were coming over until less than an hour ago. He waved her away, turned the heat down on the oven, and tented the chicken with a piece of tinfoil. Her mom put together a salad with whatever she could find—which was surprisingly abundant given that as far as I remembered, only the night before, my girlfriend and I had cleaned out the fridge for a late-night leftover meal. I was useless in the kitchen, and I stood in the doorway trying to stay out of everyone's way.

My girlfriend's mom looked up suddenly. "Where in the world is our beautiful Lamella?"

My girlfriend wagged a hand at me. "Go get Lamella and tell her to come down for dinner."

I tried to think of an excuse, but my girlfriend dropped a pot on the counter, and her mom reprimanded her for being clumsy, and they all started arguing. I went upstairs and listened outside the closed study door—there was silence on the other side.

"Dinner's almost ready," I said. There was no answer. I rapped on the door, and started to repeat myself, when it opened.

The girl looked out at me from the dark. "My mouth hurts," it said.

"What do you mean?" I asked.

"It hurts," it said, and it opened the hole at the bottom of its face. I peered inside at its rows of white teeth, which were the same shade as its white gums and its rutted white tongue. In the back, wriggling up from its throat, was a cluster of white, squirming tendrils.

I stepped back and exhaled. "Why don't you come downstairs and let someone else take a look."

The girl stepped into the hall, its naked body casting a pale shadow across the floor. I followed it downstairs to the kitchen, where my girlfriend's parents dropped whatever they were doing and embraced the girl. They planted kisses on each hole of its face. My girlfriend smiled and draped her arms around me. I watched a pot on the stove spewing steam and flecks of oil, wondering if someone should be tending to it.

I was struck by the sheer quantity of food, which I had not realized we'd had on hand. My girlfriend's dad took enormous helpings of everything, until his plate overflowed onto the table. My girlfriend's mom made a comment about this, and the two bickered casually for a minute until my girlfriend interrupted them to remark about *my* father, whose wife had just had another baby. This they already knew, but my girlfriend insisted on passing around her phone for them to look at pictures of the baby girl, who was six or seven months old. They cooed and gushed at the pictures, and asked me how I felt about it. I said it was all very exciting, but I rarely saw them, and I was used to it by now, since this was my father's and stepmom's fourth child in only six years. My girlfriend's dad slapped the table. "Four kids!" he said. "Can you imagine? He's a masochist!" And everyone laughed.

As we ate, I thought about my father and his family. What might they be doing at this moment? Were they all eating dinner together? What was that scene like? Did the nannies and nurses eat with them? And if they weren't eating, then what might they be doing instead? Were they all in the same room? Or different rooms? Did the kids all get along with each other? They were still so young, the oldest having just turned six, so I imagined it was too early to tell if they got along or not, too early for them to be anything except children. I thought about my stepmom, who was young herself—closer to my age than my father's age—and I wondered if this was a different life than she had planned for herself, or *how* different it was from what she had planned for herself, since nothing ever happened the way any of us planned.

My girlfriend's parents were asking me about my mom, my actual mom. I told them she was fine, that we had spoken recently—though as I said this I realized it was not true, that I had received a voicemail from her and never called back—but that she was fine, as far as I knew. I started to add that I worried about her sometimes, that she spent so much time alone. But I forked some chicken into my mouth instead. My girlfriend's mom asked me about work, and I shrugged and said it was stressful, and that I didn't really feel like talking about it. So they changed the subject and talked about a family friend of theirs, who I didn't know, and then about five minutes later —maybe on account of the wine—it turned out I actually *did* feel like talking about work, so I cut into the conversation. "I caught a student of mine plagiarizing," I said.

My girlfriend poked at her salad. "You didn't tell me about this," she said.

"I thought I did."

She shook her head, started to say something else, paused, then glanced at the girl. "Lamella," she said. "Why aren't you eating?"

"My mouth hurts," the girl bleated.

"What do you mean?"

"It hurts everywhere in my mouth."

"Open," said my girlfriend.

The girl opened its hole and my girlfriend took its chin in her hand, turned its face up to the light, and peered into the hole. "You look fine," she said.

"Let me look," my girlfriend's mom said, taking the girl's chin and peering into its hole. "I don't see anything wrong," she said.

I set my fork down and reached for the wine, which was nearly empty. I felt suddenly out of place —although I was among people I typically enjoyed spending time with. But in that moment I didn't want to be with them, and started formulating excuses in my head to leave, to go upstairs and shut myself in my study...Though I no longer had a study, so even if I managed to create a convincing excuse to leave the table, there was nowhere for me to go.

"So tell us about this student of yours," my girlfriend's dad said.

I finished my wine and gave my girlfriend a look that I hoped conveyed the need for another bottle, though she didn't seem to read me. "Well, he turned in a paper," I said. "About a week ago. And—and I really am certain of this, completely one hundred percent certain—the paper had very obviously been written by someone else. I mean I've seen his other work, his earlier papers, and it's like night and day. It was *too* good. I'm not even sure *I* could have written it."

"So what happened?"

"Well, I went through all the proper channels. I ran it through the school's plagiarism checker, though it came back clean. But this just means someone wrote it for him, rather than, you know, him downloading it off the internet or copying it from somewhere. And I reported my suspicions to the dean," I lifted my empty wine glass, set it down, "who's investigating it now. But meanwhile, the student has gone out of his way to make things difficult. He accused me of being unfair, and he said that the school had, like, biases or something. And today, just this afternoon, when I was leaving campus, he approached me…and he threatened me."

"*What?*" my girlfriend thumped her forearms on the table.

"Yeah. I mean, it wasn't, like, explicit. But he accosted me and said that he *had* written the paper and he deserved credit for it. And there were these guys with him, like five or six big guys, and they kind of flanked me while he was saying this stuff, just like *this* close to me…" I felt my face warm as I gestured with my hand. I wiped my mouth with my sleeve.

"What did you do?" my girlfriend asked.

"Nothing. I stood there. I didn't say anything, I just waited for him to finish. And then he and his friends walked off."

"You mean his goons," my girlfriend's dad said, shaking his head.

"You need to report him," said my girlfriend.

"I guess I do," I said. "But I don't know, I mean, yeah. I don't know."

"What don't you know?" she said. "He can't go around threatening faculty members. He should be arrested."

I nodded slowly, as if deep in thought about this. "Is there another bottle in the kitchen?" I asked, starting to get up.

"I don't think so," my girlfriend picked up her own wine glass. "But you can check."

I headed toward the kitchen, desperate to vacate the room even temporarily. But there was a sound, a clink, like a coin falling from a pocket to a floor. I looked over—we all looked over—at the girl, its hand raised slightly, the big hole at the bottom of its face hanging open, and on its plate lay a tooth. The root was intact so that it looked like a slug or a worm, and it trembled there, reflecting the light from the ceiling.

"Make a wish!" my girlfriend's dad said.

My girlfriend smiled warmly and caressed the girl's head. "My sweet Lamella," she said. "You lost your first tooth."

The girl picked up the tooth and held it near its eye holes, studying it intently. When I'd lost my own teeth as a child, it hadn't been like that, the whole tooth from the root. Mine had come out in little nubs, and there was always blood and tears.

"That's a nice-looking tooth," my girlfriend's dad said. "I'll bet the tooth fairy pays a fortune for it."

The girl's eyes rolled in a circle. It set the tooth on the table next to its plate and crossed its arms over its chest. I started again for the kitchen, but there was another clank, and another long tooth quivering on the plate. Then another clank, and another tooth, and another. And another. And then there were teeth raining from the girl's hole, clattering on the plate in a messy white pile.

My girlfriend wiped her eye and smiled. "You're growing up so fast," she said.

"This is how it happens," my girlfriend's mom said, touching my girlfriend's arm.

I chewed my lip. "Is this normal?" I muttered, though I wasn't sure anyone heard me until my girlfriend's dad responded.

"What, you never lost your baby teeth?" he said.

"We used to call them milk teeth," my girlfriend's mom said.

"You're gonna be rich!" said my girlfriend's dad as the teeth spilled from the girl's face like insects from a split in a rotted log. The plate overflowed. I tried to count them but there were too many—fifty, a hundred of them. The sound they made—the chatter of enamel on enamel—grated at my ears and made me want to run or scream. I went to the kitchen and out through the sliding doors into the back yard. I breathed the cold nighttime air in through my nose, and out through my mouth, and I tasted blood that I'd drawn from chewing the inside of my lip.

Terraces of silver clouds lumbered silently through the sky, cracking apart here and there to disclose bloated, noxious stars that hurt my eyes. A plane signaled its way below the clouds until it disappeared behind the cadaverous branches of the oak tree that had, over the last few years, grown rapidly out from beneath the corner of the house, warping sideways so that it appeared slumped, as if drunk. I gazed into the shadows of grass and bramble that separated our property from our neighbors', and I thought I saw something skulking there, a cat or a possum, but then there was only stillness.

I got cold and returned to the house. My girlfriend and her parents were clearing the dishes from the table. My girlfriend's mom was telling an amusing story about something that had happened in my girlfriend's childhood, and they all laughed. The teeth had been arranged in a line across the table, nearly from one end to the other, and everyone was careful not to disturb the teeth. The girl sat, its eyes scuttling around the room.

I positioned myself by the sink in the kitchen and received the dirty plates, rinsed them, and put them in the dishwasher. At one point my girlfriend paused to kiss me, and she tasted like the food we'd just eaten. "Thank you" she mouthed silently and walked away. I had no idea what I was being thanked for, and I made a note to ask her later, when we were alone, though I predicted I would forget.

Once everything was cleaned, we congregated in the den. My girlfriend and her mom sat on either side of the girl, stroking its hair. My girlfriend's dad paced, rubbing his full belly. I considered excusing myself to the bedroom, genuinely exhausted, my eyelids drooping as if engorged with blood. I kept expecting that my girlfriend's parents would announce that they were leaving, and I could say goodnight and see them out like an attentive host. But they made no such announcement, and finally, resigned to get it over with, I yawned deeply, and stretched my arms out to either side, and started to say that I was going upstairs. But before I could, the girl croaked, "I wanna go to bed."

My girlfriend's parents mewed and kissed the holes in its face. "We don't want to keep you up," my girlfriend's dad said. They made their goodbyes; as they were leaving, my girlfriend's dad paused at the door. "Don't forget to put those teeth under your pillow, Lamella," he called out, winking at me, and I closed and locked the door.

"That was nice," my girlfriend said.

"It was," I said, yawning.

"Let's get this one upstairs," she gestured at the girl, which was slouched over on the sofa, its white hair pooling in its lap. "Why don't you get the teeth off the table," and then she lowered her voice to a whisper. "Just put them in a box or something and hide them in the basement."

I wondered why we didn't just throw them away, but said nothing. I found a red shoebox in the hall closet and stood at the table, listening to the pair of staggered footsteps on the stairs. I examined the line of teeth and began picking them up one at a time before resorting to scooping them into the box with the outside of my hand. They made a grating sound as they slid across the table, which made my forearms break out into gooseflesh.

I set the box on a high shelf in the basement and turned off the lights on my way upstairs. The study door was shut. In the bedroom, my girlfriend sat on the bed with her legs crossed. I undressed and put my head in her lap.

"Long day," she said, stroking my hair.

I sighed. "I feel a little shaken up."

"From this whole thing with your student?"

"I guess so. I just need the weekend to get my head on straight." I looked up at her. "It is *actually* the weekend this time, right?"

"Yes, love," she leaned down and kissed my forehead. My eyes slid closed, the weight of my body sinking into the bed and the weight of my head into her warm thighs. When we'd first started dating, the tension and magnetism between us was so profound that we were afraid to release it by consummating, afraid nothing could ever be better than the wanting. So we would lie close, just like this, with my head in her lap, in silence, only touching, an intimacy without intercourse, and we would savor the ache. A shape started to form in my mind, pale and faraway. It turned and bent itself toward me, materialized, became familiar. Then there was something else, an event that unfolded to me, a series of actions. But before I could grasp their significance my girlfriend slid out from beneath me, and my head thumped onto the mattress, and I was awake again.

I blinked around. "What happened?"

She was digging through her wallet. "You need to put money under Lamella's pillow," she said. "My dad put that thought in her head and she'll be disappointed now if it's not there in the morning... Thanks, Dad." She held up a bill. "I only have a twenty."

I propped myself up on my forearms. For some reason my thoughts churned their way to an image of Samanta Sewenger walking away from me in the lobby of the Academic Center.

"Be quiet," my girlfriend said. "Don't wake her up."

My head was heavy. I considered saying something about how *she* should be the one to deposit the money, since *she* was the one who cared about it at all. But I was too tired to argue, and figured it would take less energy to just get up and get it over with than it would to start an argument. I hauled myself off the bed and down the hall. At the study door I realized I was naked. I yawned so deeply that my jaw popped, and opened the door soundlessly. The room was dark, and as I tiptoed into the darkness I heard a scraping sound, which, after a second, I determined must be the radiator. There was only a tangle of shadows on the bed. The room felt larger than I remembered it when it held my bookshelves and my desk and my reading chair. I made it to the bed without creaking a single floorboard, and peered down at the dark mass there, trying to determine where the edge of the pillow was, and how best to secure the bill beneath it. But I paused when I realized that the scraping sound was not coming from the radiator behind me—it was in fact coming from the bed, and I held the money in the dark, unsure how to proceed. And all at once the sheets rushed away, and there was a white body, and I beheld the dilated holes in its face, the glassy eyes and the toothless mouth, and the legs were spread apart, a white hand rummaging between them, scraping, and I looked off into the dark, and looked back, and covered myself with a hand.

"I'm sorry…" I said.

A gravelly voice hissed. "Get *out!*"

I fled, dropping the money on the floor and slamming the study door behind me. I rushed down the hall into the soft light of the bedroom.

"What happened?" my girlfriend asked.

I lay down beside her. "Nothing," I said. "Everything's fine."

My girlfriend squeezed my shoulder. Air seeped from her lips. A minute later she shut off the light and I lay in the dark, blinking my way to sleep, and when I awoke in the morning I was alone in the bed, feeling as if I hadn't slept at all.

There was no one downstairs, and through the window I saw my girlfriend's car was gone. I brewed a pot of coffee and stood by the sliding doors in the kitchen, gazing out at the overcast morning, trying to decide what to do with the day. Just a couple years ago I would spend Saturday mornings in my study, writing. A cup of coffee on my desk, my mind still firing along the dreamy pathways of sleep, an entire empty day sprawled ahead, inviting me to be swept up in inspiration. Beckoning me to inscribe that inspiration across pages and pages until the day swallowed shut and interred the inscription to time, to eternity, and became something important, something bigger than me. Something that *meant* something. But those days were behind me, and the hope of creating something bigger than myself, something that would outlive me, was gone, and it was never coming back.

I checked my e-mail. I had a message from Dean Oresco, informing me that a decision on the matter of my plagiarism accusation against Carl Jones—and on Carl Jones's counteraccusations against me—would be reached by Monday morning. I sat in the den and blinked at my reflection in the dark glass of the television. The remote was across the room on the television stand, and I could think of nothing I wanted to watch anyway. I considered trying to read, to read a book from beginning to end like I used to, a book that wasn't part of the college's English curriculum. Something trenchant, challenging, something that left big questions suspended in space, beating like hearts, questions that I could carry around and ponder for the rest of my life...But my books had been moved from my study, and I didn't know where they were. I sipped my coffee and eyed the remote, willing it to cross the room to my hand.

I heard a car roll into the driveway, and doors opening and slamming. Raised voices approached the house. I felt the impulse to flee, before anyone came in, upstairs to the bedroom or through the kitchen and into the back yard. But I didn't make the decision to act upon that impulse quickly enough. The front door opened and my girlfriend and a white, naked teenager whorled in, laden with shopping bags. My girlfriend was scowling, and the teenager's holes were contorted in anger.

"You're such a bitch!" the teenager seethed.

"You can't talk to me like that!" my girlfriend threw the bags down and leveled a finger at the teenager.

The teenager cocked its hips and crossed its arms impetuously over the small lumps of its breasts. I averted my eyes from its clump of white pubic hair. "You never let me do anything," it growled.

"Never let you *do* anything?" my girlfriend threw up her hands. The streaks of gray in her dark hair glistened. They noticed me then, and they both regarded me angrily, as if whatever they were fighting about was somehow my fault.

"What's going on?" I asked, finding it difficult to maintain eye contact with either of them.

"She won't let me get my lip pierced," said the teenager.

"It's asinine. You're too young," said my girlfriend.

"It's my body. I can do what I want to it." As it spoke, I noticed that the large hole at the bottom of its face was crowded with wide, white teeth. "Besides, I can pay for it myself, so it's really none of your business."

My girlfriend exhaled forcefully toward the ceiling, rubbing her temples; I noticed the creases around her eyes. "Apparently she's been saving up for this stupid piercing," she said before turning back to the teenager. "But it doesn't matter, because you aren't old enough to get it without parental consent."

"I will be soon," said the teenager, and its eyes diverged, crossed, tumbled.

My girlfriend scoffed, then turned to me. "Will you please say something?"

I raised my palms outward. "I don't want any trouble," I said, absorbing my girlfriend's glare. I turned to the teenager. "But of course she's right, you're too young." My mind was reeling with an onslaught of thoughts and questions—though I knew that to vocalize any of them would reveal to my girlfriend, and to myself, a grave misunderstanding on my part, and after this past week I could not stand to suffer additional humiliation.

The teenager clomped up the stairs. A door slammed overhead. My girlfriend's shoulders slumped. "She hates me," she said, dropping onto the sofa beside me.

I put my hand on the back of her neck. "Nobody hates you," I said.

My girlfriend rubbed her face. "I think I hate *her*…" She shook her head. "I can't believe I just said that. Of course I don't hate her. It's just, I think the worst part is just how fast everything is going. It's like just yesterday she was a baby, and she needed me, and now she needs me less and less and I feel useless and old." She lurched forward, covering her face with her hands. I stroked the back of her neck, looking at my reflection in the television. Footsteps pattered overhead and my initial thought was that I needed to go upstairs and calm Olive down before she knocked something over or scratched up the floor. But Olive was dead, she was not upstairs, and it didn't matter that I missed her—whatever *was* upstairs, scrambling across my study, was outside my jurisdiction, and if it knocked something over or scratched the floor, it could not be held accountable, and the only one to blame was myself.

"Listen," I said to my girlfriend. "Why don't you get out of the house for a while this afternoon. Go get a massage or, I don't know, go see a friend or something. Just take some time for yourself. I'll be fine here, and you'll feel better after."

My girlfriend's eyes flickered, not really seeing me. "Yeah. Yeah, I think I will. Thank you." She kissed me. "Yeah, I'm going to get out of here." She kissed me again, gathered her things, and paused only briefly at the front door to smile back at me before leaving.

I straightened up the house. I took out the garbage, swept the kitchen floor and the dining room floor and ran the dishwasher. I moved some laundry around in the basement, then decided to get really crazy and vacuum between the cushions on the sofa in the den. I vacuumed under the sofa, wiped the windows down—including the sliding doors in the kitchen—changed a light bulb in the downstairs hallway, and cleaned the stove. When there was nothing left to clean, I had no choice but to go to the study and grade papers. Except, again, the study was gone, so I sat on the sofa and spread the papers on the coffee table. I felt amateurish and feared my notes to my students reflected that amateurism. 'Sentence unclear, re-write.' 'This thesis statement not great.' 'Consider moving this paragraph.' I feared I was being useless to them, so gave nothing lower than a B. I finished the first batch of papers around noon and poured a tepid cup of coffee, then sipped it while gazing out the sliding doors at the overcast sky. My toes and fingertips were cold, so I turned up the thermostat, microwaved my coffee, and went upstairs to get a sweater from the bedroom.

The study door was shut, and there was a rustling sound behind it, like paper being torn or crinkled. I pressed my ear to the door. I heard more rustling, and a soft, deep breathing. I chewed my lip. I raised my hand to knock, but hesitated, listening, and then committed, and knocked on the door. The rustling stopped. I knocked again. An abrading voice called out, "Hold on!" I heard movement, and a different voice, a *deeper* voice, and the scraping of furniture. I threw open the door. The teenager was sitting on the bed with the sheets pulled up to its neck. Behind it, halfway through the open window, a boy clambered away, his pants unfastened and falling around his waist, his shirt and coat clutched in one hand.

"Hey!" I shouted, storming across the room.

"Leave him alone!" the teenager barked.

I scrabbled across the bed and lunged for the boy —but he was already outside, shimmying down the trunk of the oak tree. He leapt the final ten feet, landing hard, and looked back up at me as I craned my neck out the window. His face was familiar, I thought, though I could not place it. He turned and sprinted around the side of the house. A few seconds later a car engine exploded to life, and the screech of tires faded into the distance.

I drew myself from the open window and in a furious rush I slammed the window shut. I turned on the teenager. "Who the *fuck* was that?"

It looked back at me with huge, horrified eyes. The holes in its face pulsed, and it clutched the sheets around its neck. I breathed in through my nose and blew a thin line of air out through my teeth.

I sat down on the edge of the bed. "Who was that?" I asked again, calmly.

"Just some boy," croaked the teenager. Its holes grimaced, and it shifted its weight under the sheets. "It's not a big deal."

I scoffed. "It *is* a big deal. This is *my* house. I won't have people coming in and out of windows." I glanced down at the white sheets, the same color as the teenager's skin, and there were patches of little white flakes, like snow, scattered across them. The teenager shifted uncomfortably, its big teeth bared. "Are you okay?" I asked.

"My stomach hurts," it rasped. The holes in its face clenched. It dropped a hand to its abdomen, and the sheet fell away to reveal one of its large, nipple-less breasts. It heaved forward and made a terrible, metallic coughing sound. I almost reached out to it, impulsively.

I stood up. "Can I get you something? Some water?" I asked.

It lurched again. Another pained sound escaped it, and both of its hands clenched at its stomach. It fell onto its back and kicked its legs, displacing the sheets. Beneath its hands the flat part of its belly protruded, as if filling with air. It rocked side to side, curled its toes and bellowed. I knelt beside the bed and touched its dry skin, trying to think of what to do, or what to say to give it some solace. Its belly ballooned upward into a dome, and it flailed its legs apart and balled its hands at its crotch. Its eyes jutted from the holes in its face. Unthinking, I crawled to the foot of the bed and looked between its legs. There were more holes there. I tried to count them but there were too many. One of them, the biggest one, fluttered and dilated, and from within it emerged a dark shape, a startling contrast to the white of the teenager's skin. It bulged from the hole, expanding it perilously, and the white skin cracked. I expected it to bleed, but there was no blood, just more dry white. I reached out, and cupped my hands, and guided the dark, matted head from the white hole. There followed a cramped pair of shoulders, and a narrow, purple body, and feet tangled in a white, varicose cord. After that spilled a rumpled white sac—like a wad of paper—onto the mattress.

I stood, holding the baby. My hands shook. "It's a boy," I said, impulsively. I held it toward the teenager, who breathed heavily, the holes in its face spreading open. When its eyes beheld the baby, it cooed. And in that moment, its voice, for once, was not grating, but was smooth, and breathy, and pleasant. It reached for the baby, which seemed already larger than it had just a moment before. I placed him in its arms and drew the sheets up to cover it. It held the baby boy to its chest and gazed at him with wonder and adoration. The baby's eyes opened—his eyes were huge and glassy—and he looked around, at the teenager, at me, at the white room. The cord extending from his belly cracked off then and withered into a thin twig. The teenager squeezed the baby between its breasts. Except he was too large, and he weighed down on them, and he flopped over onto the bed beside the teenager, which clenched his thickening wrist in its hand. Brown hair sprouted from the baby's head, and his legs and arms lengthened until they dangled off the edge of the bed. I stepped back, smelling iron and soil. The boy's face slimmed as his hair grew, spilling on the bed. His fingers and toes elongated, his torso bulkened, and he rolled off the side of the bed, thudding onto the floor. The teenager gasped and reached for him. He lay there protracting and filling, his eyes tumbling in circles. Hair sprouted around his groin and his chin and from his armpits and across his chest. His skin grew coarse, and a sputtering, snapping sound issued from him—or so I thought, until a moment later I realized it was coming from the radiator behind me. The teenager reached down and touched his chest, the holes in its face contorting into angles of despair. The boy, now as large as me, rippled and quaked, his skin contracting around his ribs and folding at his eyes, and the graying hair from his head and his face pooled around the floor. His knuckles swelled and his limbs tautened, and veins showed through his papery skin. His eyes skipped around the room, desperate— no longer seeing, I thought, but searching. And then the eyes stopped moving, and the body seemed to constrict in on itself. The hair stopped growing, and the flesh stiffened and paled and calcified around the bones and folded inward, collapsing. It dried and flaked and broke apart into small pieces, and then into larger pieces, and those larger pieces into smaller pieces until there was no indication of a person but instead a pile of gray sand, which shivered in the white room, and turned to dust which rose up on the warm air from the radiator, dispersed, and was gone.

I blinked down at the empty space on the floor. I blinked up at the teenager. Its face was clenched, its holes squarish. I tried to swallow but there was no saliva. When I spoke, my voice came out in a choked whisper. "Are you okay?"

It looked up at me. Its eyes were set far back in its holes. "Please don't tell Mom," it said, its voice again raspy and dry.

The radiator moaned. I wracked my brain for something to do, for some action or gesture. I picked up the empty glass from the bedside table, filled it with water from the bathroom, and returned it. The young woman was on its side, with the sheets drawn over its head, unmoving. I glanced out the window at the braided branches of the oak tree, and the silver sky. I left the room, shutting the door gently behind me.

I showered—for the first time in days, I realized, only after I was standing under the water. I considered shaving, but the task seemed daunting, so I dressed and went downstairs. The coffee table was a mess, strewn with half-graded papers. I arranged them vaguely into a pile. My stomach complained. I rummaged through the fridge and through various cabinets but found nothing appealing. I pulled my cold coffee from the microwave and sat on the sofa with my legs drawn up in a manner that I suspected —if anyone had been watching—would have made me appear younger than I was. I wondered how old I appeared to people generally. I wondered how old Samanta Sewenger thought I was. She probably knew my age, since she had access to the records the school kept on those things. I wondered how old *she* was. I guessed at most mid-thirties, though much more likely late twenties, and probably not much younger than twenty-six. I wondered what she might be doing right now, on this overcast Saturday afternoon. Certainly it had nothing to do with me or the school's investigation into my plagiarism allegations against Carl Jones. Ultimately, I assumed, she had little or nothing to do with the investigation itself, or the final decision. I tried to imagine what that investigation looked like, at this moment. Were Dean Oresco and a panel of administrators poring over Carl's papers? Were they seeking inconsistencies or identifying evidence of impropriety on my part? Did they bring someone in to examine syntax, grammatical patterns, punctuation usage, in order determine the papers' authors? Of course not. Such things were reserved for criminal investigations and the like. But I wondered what then, exactly, they *were* doing to verify or disprove my claims.

I considered e-mailing Dean Oresco to inquire about the process that would determine my fate. It was, after all, my right to know how I was being judged, so that I could better defend myself. But I decided such an inquiry might appear spurious, and that such an appearance might indicate that I believed I had done something wrong. I decided instead to e-mail Samanta Sewenger, to ask what *she* thought I could be doing in the meantime to help myself, since she had after all expressed some amount of solidarity, and I considered her an ally. I pictured her crawling under the table and unbuckling my pants, her mouth curling, her dark hair framing her slender face—and I shifted my weight on the couch. And because I didn't know where my laptop was, I used my phone to search the college's faculty/staff directory for Samanta Sewenger's e-mail address, and wrote to her on my phone.

'Dear Samanta,

Firstly, I want to apologize for the other day. I really meant nothing other than what I said, and I am embarrassed by the misunderstanding. I hope it will not negatively impact our professional relationship, or negatively color your opinion about me or my professional integrity and commitment to my students.

But that is not why I am writing. I am aware that a decision will be reached by Monday concerning the administration's findings in the matter involving Carl Jones. I feel left in the dark, somewhat, as to the process of this investigation (Who exactly is investigating? How are they going about it?) and I was hoping that you might be willing and able to shed some light here for me. I considered e-mailing Dean Oresco about this, but do not want to appear as if I am trying to interfere. If you think it is more appropriate that I e-mail the dean, please let me know, and I will do that.

Thank you for your time. I apologize, again, for the misunderstanding.

Sincerely,

Mel Lane'

I sent it before I could change my mind, and immediately suspected I'd made a mistake. I reread it, trying to determine its *actual* message, the message Samanta might glean from it. But it was too late. I had sent it, and there was nothing more I could do.

I heard movement upstairs. The shower ran, and water rushed through the pipes in the walls. I was confused for a moment because I thought my girlfriend was out. But then I remembered the young woman, and everything that had just happened. I shook my head quickly, as if to cast it away, since it was over. It was in the past.

I went upstairs and peeked into the study. The sheets were flayed from the mattress in a heap on the floor, and the blinds on both windows were closed so only thin slats of gray light bled through. I listened to the patter of the shower down the hall, trying to remember how the study had looked when my desk and bookshelves and reading chair were still in it. I couldn't quite figure it out, because the walls seemed wider than I remembered, and I couldn't see how my reading chair had fit into the corner where the radiator was, or how my desk had been flush against the right wall when that wall was so clearly slanted. The windows further confused me. I distinctly remembered only one window, though now there were two, side-by-side. And the ceiling had a light fixture in it, though I had memories of shopping for lamps when we'd first moved in, to light the room, which my girlfriend joked was the dungeon I'd always dreamed of writing in.

The shower abruptly turned off and I scampered to the bedroom and shut the door. I heard the bathroom door open, and the floorboards in the hall creak. I sat on the bed and busied myself on my phone. The creaking paused halfway down the hall, then continued toward the bedroom. There was a knock on the door, hesitant, arrhythmic. I flopped onto my back, closed my eyes, and pretended to sleep. The door opened slowly, and through the creases of my eyes I saw the young woman, its skin so white it seemed to cast its own light, its torso wrapped in a towel and its white hair damp and slicked back from its face. Its holes were bare and puckered, and its eyes were enormous.

It stood at the doorway. "Hello?" it croaked.

I focused on keeping my breath measured. Saliva pooled in the ditch of my throat.

The young woman entered the bedroom, shutting the door behind it. It walked to the bed and stood over me. I felt its cool shadow fall over my face, and I pretended to stir slightly, twitching one of my feet, inhaling deeply through my nose. I pressed my eyes completely closed.

The bed sagged. I felt the young woman climb over me and lay down beside me. It pressed against the side of my body, smelling like soap—and, beneath the soap, dirt and copper. It nestled its head into the pillow, draped its arm over my chest. It exhaled, its breath rattling, and a clump of its damp hair tumbled onto my cheek and coiled there. I continued to focus on breathing slowly, and I listened to the young woman's breathing which synced with mine within a few minutes—whether by coincidence or by design (mine or its). It nestled closer to me, so that its face wedged against my neck, and it tightened its arm around me and stretched a bare leg over my legs, so that if we were vertical it would have appeared to be climbing me. Its weight on my body was soothing, and my thoughts glided downward into the marshes and woodlands of sleep, circling the strange, skinless object of dreams. My eyes opened once, when I thought I heard something move in the house, but then it was quiet, and the young woman breathed beside me, its body hoisted half atop mine, and as far as I could tell it was asleep too.

I dreamed that I stood on the bank of a wide, dry river. An enormous suspension bridge spanned the river's width, and near the bridge's middle was a gaping hole as if a bomb had gone off. The pale metal was twisted and charred, and I knew I was responsible for that hole, and I knew there were people after me, to punish me for it, and I was filled with dread that I would be caught and incarcerated. But I did nothing but stand on the riverbank and look at the bridge, the sky a sheet of white clouds, and the whole earth seemed to lurch beneath it, to carry me and the bridge and the dry river along. I worried about where we were going, and how long it would take, and whether I knew anyone who would be there when we arrived. There was movement to my left, a shifting of space, and the light changed, and my eyes blinked apart and I looked up at the crack in the ceiling over the bed, which ran from one side to the other. Behind it was white plaster, the same color as the paint. There was something in the doorway, a dark shape, toward which I dragged my eyes. My girlfriend, with one hand on the doorknob and the other drifting near the light switch. Her eyes darted over me and the young woman—which slept, its breathing slow, its body cocooned around mine. Its towel had been cast aside, and at some point while I slept my arm had shifted so that it encircled the young woman's back, and my hand rested on the edge of its breast. I raised my head and looked at my girlfriend, and I tried to smile, to show that nothing was wrong. She turned and stamped down the hall, leaving the bedroom door open. The young woman stirred, raised its head; the holes in its face spread open, and its eyes toppled around the room and settled on me. Its holes seemed to smile sleepily, and I smiled back.

The television went on downstairs. I slid my arm out from beneath the young woman, which had drifted back to sleep, and closed the bedroom door behind me. At the top of the stairs, I felt blood pulse in my feet. My head swam momentarily. I glanced down at my shirt and found that I was covered in white specks. I wiped at them as I went downstairs to the den.

My girlfriend did not look at me when I entered. She glared at the television, her legs crossed firmly, her foot bobbing up and down. As I sat beside her she said, without looking at me, "What the hell was that?"

I frowned, shrugged. "What was what? I was taking a nap."

"That looked like more than a nap," she said, her mouth twisting.

"I don't understand," I said, though I felt my face get warm.

My girlfriend rolled her eyes. We sat and looked at the television. My thoughts sputtered. "So, what did you do today?" I said finally.

"Nothing," she said.

"Where did you go? How'd you spend the afternoon?"

She was silent.

Exasperation welled up in my chest and into my throat and out of my mouth. "What exactly is the matter? Are you *jealous* of something?"

She sat forward, and her face blistered into hurt and rage. Her mouth opened, and I anticipated yelling, hurtful accusations, things drudged up. But her mouth closed, her eyes softened, and she leaned back. "I just miss you," she said, and there was so much weight in her voice. "I miss being with you, the way it used to be before Lamella, before you were working all the time. When we were, you know, swept up in each other." She sniffled, wiped her eyes. "Seeing you two like that, just lying there together, it reminded me of everything you and I used to have, and everything we don't have anymore."

I slid close to her and put my arms around her. Her hair smelled different than usual. I kissed her. "My love," I said. "We have our whole lives ahead of us. There's nothing that can get in the way of that. The way I feel about you, the love I have for you, it grows every day. I know things have changed, and that I've been busy and…maybe a little distant. But we can—*I* can work on that. You deserve the best I can give you."

She smiled, though her eyes were sad. We kissed, and her lips were soft and dry and she tasted like vanilla.

"How about tonight I take you out for dinner," I said. "We can go to that place by the river, the one with the big fireplace."

"Yeah?"

"Oh yeah. Come on, let's get ready. We'll get there early, have some drinks and watch the sunset."

"It's cloudy out."

"We'll watch the clouds then. Come on." I stood and hauled her up by her arms. She giggled and we kissed again. She pushed her hair back, turned in a circle. She ran upstairs to shower, and I followed her and stood in the bathroom and watched her. She wiped a plop of shampoo on my nose and laughed, and I turned the faucet to cold and she squealed and tossed handfuls of cold water at me. When she got out I dried her off, and we stood in the bathroom kissing, the towel on the floor and the door wide open—there was a sound in the hall and we looked, but there was no one. In the bedroom I pretended to be a flamboyant fashion designer—dressing her, my model, for a fabulous event. I threw clothes at her from her closet and snapped my fingers and sucked my teeth and commanded her to try on all manner of ridiculous outfits. Eventually she wound up in a beautiful puce dress and black boots, and I changed into a collared shirt and put a sweater over it.

She kissed me with her tongue. "Mm, Professor," she said. "How'd I do on my test?"

"You're going to need to do a little extra credit," I said, deepening my voice. "Otherwise I'm gonna have to give you a big ol' F."

We laughed uproariously and headed down the hall to the stairs. My girlfriend paused outside the door to the study. "Lamella," she knocked once. "Your father's taking me out to dinner." There was silence from the other side. My girlfriend shrugged and took my arm. We turned off the lights as we went, locked the front door behind us, and drove off toward the river.

At the restaurant we sat at the bar while we waited to be seated and ordered drinks. As soon as they arrived my phone rang. "It's my mom," I said.

"Answer it," said my girlfriend. "When's the last time you spoke to her?"

"I'll call her back," I returned the phone to my pocket. "Now, where were we?"

We toasted and gazed at each other. She was gorgeous. Other men in the restaurant were watching her from the corners of their eyes, which made me feel proud and powerful.

"We haven't been here in forever," my girlfriend said. "Over a year."

"It doesn't feel that long," I sipped my drink.

A family ate at a table toward the center of the restaurant, a mother and father and three boys. The father leaned across the table to cut the youngest boy's steak into smaller pieces. The boy watched intently, studying this procedure as if he expected he'd need to replicate it later on. The mother stroked the middle child's hair. The oldest shoveled spaghetti into his mouth. They all looked alike, even the mother and father, and when I glanced at my girlfriend I saw her watching them too, and her lips seemed to mouth a word over and over.

I reached out and put my hand on hers. "Do you want that?" I asked.

She looked at me, surprised, as if she'd forgotten I was there. "Maybe, someday," she said. "Why don't we worry about one thing at a time."

I kissed her hand. We were seated at a table near the stone mantle, as per our request, and ordered more drinks. We chatted about nothing and about everything. She revealed that she was considering going back to school to study massage, which was something she'd always wanted to do. With nothing else in her way, there was no reason to let any more time slip by. I told her this sounded like a great idea, and that I would help her however I could. She said these massage programs could be very expensive, and that she would get very busy and would need my help keeping the house in order. I told her I would do my best, and then I asked, "How expensive?" She said it could cost twenty thousand or more for the whole program, and that she had a little saved away but might need some help. I told her I would help with what I could. I imagined Samanta Sewenger on the phone with Dean Oresco, accusing me of harassment, and I remembered that I had e-mailed Samanta earlier and was expecting an e-mail back. I excused myself to the bathroom and checked my e-mail, but there was nothing.

Back at the table I was distracted for a few minutes by the eerie image of Samanta Sewenger staring up at me with wide, lidless eyes from beneath the tablecloth, and I missed a whole chunk of whatever my girlfriend was talking about.

By the time our food arrived my appetite had waned, perhaps on account of the alcohol. I pushed my dinner around my plate and left most of it behind. We left the restaurant and got in the car, and I pointed us in the direction of home. "Why don't we drive around a bit," my girlfriend suggested.

"Sure," I said. "Where would you like to go?"

"It doesn't matter," she said. "I just want to spend a little more time with you."

I drove us down local roads along the river, over the serried train tracks and past the rows of warehouses and the nuclear power plant, which loomed as if in the shadow of itself. I turned the car onto a narrow road that wound through rows of storage units, and when we reached a dead end I started to turn around. "Wait," my girlfriend said, putting her hand on my arm. "Stop here for a minute." I put the car in park and we looked through the windshield at the circles of the car's headlights, which seemed to bore holes in the darkness. She reached out and took my hand. "There's something I have to tell you," she said. "I've been meaning to tell you for a long time, but it just hasn't felt like the right moment. And I need to get it out now, or else..."

"You can tell me anything," I said.

She wrung her hand in mine. "I've been taking something, for depression..." she glanced sidelong at me. "Only for a month or two. I guess it's not a big deal, I just feel like I've been hiding it from you. I've been afraid to tell you."

"Why?"

"Why what?"

"Why have you been afraid to tell me? You've taken antidepressants in the past. I've never had a problem with it. Why would I?"

"It's different this time," she looked through the dark passenger window. "It's…I've been feeling far away from you—which is part of what was making me depressed to begin with, I think. Like, I was afraid if I told you, and if I told you why, that you would think it was your fault, or that you could do something about it, which you can't."

I cracked my neck and shifted in my seat. "Well, is it working?"

"Yes. I mean, I think so. It's not just the drugs. I'm also working with my therapist, and just processing stuff on my own. And I feel good right now, I mean really happy. Tonight was…tonight was amazing. Just getting to spend time with you, it's the best. Even though…"

"Even though what?"

"Even though there's still that *something* underneath. That's the thing about depression—it kind of lurks there under everything, no matter what's going on. It never goes away. It's still here, right now, and I guess I just have to get used to it."

"I didn't realize all this was going on," I said. "I wish I'd known. I could have done something."

"No! That's what I just said. There's nothing you could do—nothing you *can* do. It's not about you at all."

"But you just said—"

"I mean, it's *about* you but not about anything you're doing. Or not about anything you're doing *wrong*. It's about *us*, or about me and my place in us. I don't know."

Traffic from the highway—running across an overpass a hundred yards ahead—rumbled like thunder.

"Anyway, I don't want to keep any secrets from you," my girlfriend said. "And when I do I feel icky, like really bad. And I've been feeling that way for months." She looked over at me, and I looked at her, and her eyebrows went up and down, as if she were trying to signal something else that she didn't want to have to say aloud.

I squeezed her hand. "Well, I'm glad you told me," I said. "And I'm glad it's working. And whatever you need me to do, or need me *not* to do, I will. Or I won't." And then I added, because it sprang to my mind, "I'm completely invested in this."

She let go of my hand and turned away. I looked at the shape of her in the dark car, the stray white hairs that haloed her head. I turned the car around— its headlights illuminated swatches of blurry concrete —and drove us home down the same local roads along the river. In the distance, blue and orange lights reflected quavering pathways on the black water. Planes blinked along the horizon at obtuse angles, as if broadcasting urgent messages. And just as I thought they were finally getting through to me, or I was finally letting them in, I turned the car away from the river, and the planes were obscured by dark homes, and I pulled the car into the driveway and shut it off. My girlfriend and I went into the house without speaking.

She went upstairs, and I heard the bedroom door click shut. I took off my shoes and wandered around downstairs, turning on lights. The three or four drinks I'd had with dinner caught up to me, and my head swam. I checked my e-mail, but there was still nothing. I stood at the two dark windows in the dining room. The plants along the windowsills were browning and limp. I heard my girlfriend come downstairs and into the room behind me. "We need to help these plants," I said, and I turned around to face her—but it wasn't my girlfriend. It was a naked woman with paper-white skin and many holes in its face, standing with its hands behind its back. The largest hole curled up at the edges.

"You said a red box, right?" it rasped.

I shook my head, not understanding.

"Your dog's urn. You said it was a red box."

"Yes."

"I found it," it said.

"You did? Where?"

"In the basement," it said. "On a high shelf." It brought its hands out from behind its back, and set a red box on the table. My heart swelled with relief. My Olive had been returned to me. I picked up the box... but something was wrong. It was too light, and it fit awkwardly in my hands. And when I lifted the lid I saw only a pile of long, white teeth.

I looked up at the woman. It watched me expectantly. I felt a warmth in my throat, something like affection, and also disappointment.

I closed the lid. "Thank you," I said.

The woman nodded and disappeared into the kitchen. Cabinets opened and closed. Pots and glasses clinked.

I went upstairs. In the bedroom, my girlfriend lay on the bed in a t-shirt and a pair of my boxers. Her hair was fastened up in a bun. She was reading a hardcover book with the jacket missing, her hand covering the spine. I slid the red box beneath the bedside table, emptied my pockets, and climbed onto the bed beside to her. "I had a really nice time tonight," I said, brushing my fingers along her thigh. She did not react, or was too swept up in her reading to notice me, which happened sometimes. I studied her profile, the curve of her forehead, the flat angle of her nose, the gentle hills of her lips and the ditch above her chin. I reached out and touched her neck, traced the vertical chords there. She shrugged me away and turned a page. I set my hands in my lap. I considered asking her what had happened, what exactly I had missed. I rolled onto my side, with my back to her, and I texted her. 'I love you.' Her phone chirped, but she ignored it. I felt heavy from the alcohol. I got up and left the room.

I glanced into the study as I passed. A bedside lamp cast a yellow circle across the white bed—neatly made—and across the white section of floor beside it. Otherwise, the room was empty. I continued downstairs, peering from room to room. In the kitchen, I searched through cabinets for something, not knowing what it was until I found it, far in the back of the cabinet over the stove. I opened it, smelled it. It was stringent, and I filled a glass halfway and leaned on the counter and sipped. I gazed at my reflection in the dark sliding doors. After nearly a minute, I realized there was something on the other side of them—a white shape, barely illuminated by the light from the kitchen. I considered slinking away, back upstairs, but I thought of my girlfriend there, occupying our bed. I fetched a second glass, filled it with scotch, and went out into the backyard.

The woman turned. Its holes opened, surprised to see me, and it seemed to smile. I smelled the iron and earth of it, and I smelled cigarette smoke. I extended one of the glasses, which it took, and we stood side by side in the cold dark, looking out at the starless night.

"I didn't know you smoked," I said.

"Only sometimes," it said, its crepitating voice muted by the cold. "It's something to do." It held out the cigarette to me. I hesitated, then took it. It had been years since I'd smoked, and I coughed and handed it back. "Delicious," I said.

"Did you have a nice dinner?" it asked.

"Yeah. It was lovely."

The woman sighed, and it sounded like small rocks cascading down a mountain. Several quiet minutes unfurled. I grew chilled, and was about to excuse myself to go inside and warm up when it spoke. "When I was a girl," it said, smoke whorling from its holes, "Mom took me to the movies. Everything that was playing was for grownups, and I remember that we almost didn't go in at all. But I pushed and pushed, because I had never seen a movie before—in a theater, I mean—and I didn't know if I would ever get another chance. I guess everything we do might be our only chance, right? Or our last chance. Even something as simple as going to the movies. Anyway, finally she relented, and we went to see the movie that she felt would be the least inappropriate. It turned out to be a comedy about a man and a woman who find a baby in the bar they work at, and through this series of outlandish circumstances end up being ordered by a judge to raise the baby together. The whole thing was raucous and full of sex jokes, and eventually the man and woman—who up until then had always just considered themselves friends and nothing more— end up falling in love and creating their own sort of little family with the baby they found. It was supposed to be heartwarming or something, but mostly it was just dirty jokes. But I remember being in the theater with Mom and watching this grownup movie, and everyone else in the theater was laughing at the jokes, including Mom. And I was sitting there, trying so hard to understand the jokes or figure out what *was* a joke and what *wasn't*. But I couldn't. I just couldn't figure it out. And I felt then, I remember, just so young and naïve, and so far away from this entire realm of knowledge, even stupid knowledge like what was funny and why. And I couldn't enjoy the movie—probably wouldn't have even if I'd understood it—but I spent the whole two hours or whatever just feeling separate from the world, from the world as it made sense to grownups, to everyone else. It was off-limits to me.

"And as a child you have no perspective on being a child—you may realize you're a child relative to grownups, but the idea that you will ever grow up, or that you will learn things, or that the world will open up to you eventually if you just hold on—these ideas never cross your mind. And so there I was, outside the joke, and everyone around me got it. And when we left the theater, I remember feeling like that outside-ness was now somehow part of me permanently, no longer just as it related to the stupid movie we saw, but now to everything. Suddenly the whole world was comprised of all these elements that exceeded my understanding, that weren't for me and never would be. I was an outcast from the punchline of the world, and the world felt scary, and it felt too large, and too far away. And all because of that dumb movie with its dumb jokes which, of course, now I realize were not all that complicated or interesting or holding any secrets—they were just jokes that I didn't get, because I was a little girl. But it was like it was too late, and the damage was done, and I walked around my whole life with that feeling, like I was too young or too naïve to understand the world the way other people understood it. And I think I still feel that to this day..." The woman lifted the cigarette to its lips, discovered it was burnt to the filter, and flicked it off into the dark.

I breathed on my fingertips to warm them. The woman gave no indication of being affected by the frigid air. I sipped the last of my scotch.

"Of course, now I realize that no one gets it," it continued. "I mean, they get the dumb jokes in movies, but they don't get what's really going on. Some people say they do, they act like they do. But they don't. Especially those people who say or act like they get it, especially *those* people...And I see now that the truth of the world to grownups is like the jokes in a raunchy sex comedy to kids. It's over their heads. They're all just laughing along so that other people think they get the joke. And if one person laughs, everyone else laughs with them, to show that they're in on it. But in reality, they don't get it, and that person who laughed to begin with was laughing at something else. Or maybe there's really no joke at all, and nothing is actually funny."

Snow appeared suddenly suspended in the air, caught in the glow of the light through the doors. I was shivering now and wanted badly to go inside. But I felt there was something left to be said, and that to leave without saying it would amount to callousness. I shut my eyes and tried to think of what I was supposed to say. For some reason I felt there was only one thing, one specific thing to be said, and that I had only one chance to get it right. I searched through my mind as if through boxes in an attic. But all I seemed to find were artifacts that signaled failure, reminders of the myriad ways I had misunderstood. I opened my eyes and turned to the woman—but it was not there. I was alone in the backyard, in the cold. I let myself inside and closed the doors behind me. I cupped my hands against the glass, squinting into the dark. Just for a moment a white shape stirred in the shadow, near the edge of the grass and bramble that lined the property. But it might only have been a pall of snow, or the reflection of my own face in the door.

My girlfriend was asleep on her back with the reading light still on. I lifted the book from her lap—I did not recognize the title or author, the letters passing through my eyes and turning to smoke—and I shut off the lights and undressed in the dark. As I lay there I thought about the snow, and how it had seemed not to be falling at all but rather locked in the air, uncommitted to its descent and wishing, perhaps, to retreat. Only now it was too late, and it found itself stuck between the sky and the earth, refusing to land, fighting to go back up. I wondered how long it could remain like that, and as I drifted off to sleep I heard footsteps in the hall, and a door close faintly, and it was as if the door closed the room of my consciousness, and sleep ensued.

I woke to light crashing through the window. I was alone. The crack along the ceiling had branched into another crack, this one perpendicular to the first. The dream I'd been having splintered apart until there was nothing left of it but a featureless nub. I hunkered in the sheets, willing it to return—though every detail of it was gone, there still lingered the trace of a desperate message, bellowed from under a thousand feet of water. I checked my phone and saw that it was after 10:00am, two hours later than I could remember sleeping in years. I had a new e-mail, which had come in a few hours earlier, and which I read under the sheets.

'Mel,

Please contact Dean Mary Oresco with any questions concerning this ongoing matter.

Samanta Sewenger

Assistant to the Dean'

I read it again, looking for where it addressed the part that mattered. I knew it was in there somewhere. I could see it peeking through. I looked inside the words, and read it acrostically, and read it backwards. But it degraded further into meaninglessness, and finally I set the phone on my chest and tried to make myself smile, but it felt demented, as if I were insane.

The smell of bacon and coffee was strong, and there were noises downstairs—voices and laughter and the clanking of plates and silverware. The study door was open, the bed inside neatly made. As I descended the stairs, I started to discern individual voices. My girlfriend's voice, speaking casually. A low voice, a man's voice, which I maybe recognized though could not identify. Children's voices, all chattering at once, and the patter of feet.

As I stepped off the stairs a boy appeared, maybe six years old. He looked just like me, I thought, but I did not recognize him. "Hi, Mel," he said, waving both hands and then running off.

A girl appeared next, younger, maybe four, her hair combed back from her face. "Hi, Mel," she said in a squeaky voice, and hugged me around the knees before running after the boy.

I passed through the dining room, which was airy and sunny, and into the kitchen. A toddler tottered toward me. There were people—too many people—looking at me and smiling. One of them, a man my height and with my face, said, "Hey, sleeping beauty!" And recognition clicked into place. My father—though I had never seen him in my kitchen, and the context was off-putting—and beside him my stepmom—who kissed me on both cheeks—holding a baby draped in long white blankets. My father shook my hand as I blinked around the bright kitchen. My girlfriend poured a cup of coffee. At the stove was an old woman, its naked, creased skin garish in the midmorning light that spilled through the sliding doors. I must have looked bemused, or in shock, because my father laughed. "Guess you forgot we were coming, huh?"

I shrugged and shook my head, and reminded myself to smile.

My girlfriend handed me a cup of coffee. "You certainly forgot to tell me," she said, and smiled with only her mouth.

"How long have you guys been here?" I asked.

"Only half an hour," said my stepmom. "Lamella has been cooking up a storm for us. Pancakes, bacon —she even made quiche, which smells amazing."

The old woman turned briefly, its holes stretched thin across its face, its eyes like fogged glass. Specks of grease leapt off the stove in acute arcs.

My father slapped my shoulder, sloshing some of the coffee onto my hand. "Not used to such a full house, huh?" he said.

"Yeah, well, I slept much later than I'm used to. And I guess I'm not used to so much, um, youthfulness." I gestured at the baby in my stepmom's arms, and the toddler warbling from the fridge to my father's legs, and at the four-year-old girl who chased the six-year-old boy through the dining room and into the den and back into the dining room, shrieking.

"You have all this to look forward to," my stepmom said, winking at my girlfriend.

My girlfriend gritted her teeth. "It's gonna take us a little while to catch up to you guys," she said, and we all laughed, though my father laughed the hardest.

My stepmom handed the baby to my father, and followed my girlfriend, carrying plates and silverware, into the dining room. My father held the baby facing away from him. He kept looking at me as if he was about to speak, but said nothing. I took gulps of my coffee, which burned my stomach, and poured myself another cup.

The six-year-old entered the kitchen, followed by the four-year-old. They tugged my father's pantlegs. "Can we go outside?" they asked.

"I don't know, what's out there?"

"It's okay," I said. "I'll go with them."

My girlfriend returned to the kitchen for another load of plates.

I opened the sliding doors and followed the kids into the backyard. It was warm, with no trace of snow from the previous night. The kids ran in circles in the grass and I stood beside the oak tree at the edge of the house, prepared to intercept them should they come this way, which led toward the road. They shouted words I did not understand, and made sounds that I decided might be lasers, though they were different than the laser sounds I used to make when I was young.

A shallow, shaky carving was etched into the trunk of the oak tree. I ran my fingers across it. 'S + L.' I had never noticed it before, but had never spent much time standing in this spot. It had likely been there forever, and I wondered what else I might be failing to notice.

"Breakfast is ready," someone called from the house, either my girlfriend or my stepmom. I shepherded the kids inside, and we all took seats around the dining room table. The baby sat limply in my stepmom's lap, and the toddler in my father's lap. My father cut his quiche into small bites. The sink ran in the kitchen, and pots clanged. The old woman was absent, and there was nowhere for it to sit. "Are we waiting?" I asked.

"Waiting for what?" my girlfriend said.

"You wanna say grace or something?" my father said, and he and my stepmom laughed.

"What's grace?" asked the six-year-old.

"Nothing," said my stepmom, and for a minute there was only the sound of silverware scraping porcelain.

My stepmom asked me about work.

"You know, same old," I said.

My girlfriend frowned. "What about the student you're having problems with?" she said. "The one who cheated."

I shook my head. "I don't think it's going to be a big deal."

"Did you tell the school that he threatened you?" my girlfriend asked.

My stepmom's eyes widened. "You were threatened by a student?"

My face warmed. "It wasn't serious. What happened was that I suspected he had plagiarized a paper, and brought it to the administration, who are now investigating it. And he, the student, found out that this was happening and he…confronted me…just to claim that he really did write the paper, and that he deserved credit for it."

"And his friends surrounded you," said my girlfriend.

"Well, yeah, kind of." I shoveled quiche into my mouth.

"So, what's going to happen?" my stepmom asked.

I chewed. The six-year-old furtively knocked a piece of the four-year-old's food onto the floor, and the four-year-old disappeared under the table to fetch it. "I'll know on Monday what the administration decides," I said. "They have all the information they need. It's out of my hands now."

"Will he get expelled?"

"Possibly," I said.

"Good," said my father. "Sounds like a real fuck-up."

"Language," my stepmom hissed, gesturing at the kids.

"Oops," my father winked at my girlfriend.

"Well, I hope it all works out for you," said my stepmom.

"Me too," I said. I wanted to say more, to say that the education system was broken, that these students were being punished for the sins of the system, and how I was worried I was becoming part of that problem. That it was so systemic and deeply rooted and so drastically exceeded the bounds of one adjunct professor or even a group of administrators. That it was an economic issue hinging on the ebb and flow of funding, and that it was the students who suffered as a result, and it was so unfair. But something grabbed my leg, and I looked down at the four-year-old, who smiled up at me from under the table. I smiled back and inserted a chunk of quiche into my mouth.

"We had dinner with your sister last night," my stepmom said.

My girlfriend tilted her head. "Who are you talking to?" she asked.

"To Mel. We had dinner with his sister at Citron last night. They changed their menu. No more coq au vin. Such a shame."

My girlfriend set her fork down and frowned at me. "You have a sister?"

My stepmom laughed. "She was saying how sad she is that she never gets to see you two. It's been over a year, she said. Is that true?"

I nodded. "Even longer," I said. "Closer to two."

My girlfriend crossed her arms. "I don't understand," she said. "I didn't know you had a sister—I mean besides these..." she gestured at the four-year-old, who was climbing back onto her chair, and at the baby in my stepmom's arms. "How did I not know you had another sister?"

"What are you talking about?" my stepmom said. "She actually said she'd spoken to you more recently than she'd spoken to Mel. She was going on about how happy she was that you were around to take care of her little brother. And she wished she got to see you guys more."

"How long is she in the city?" I asked.

"Just until Wednesday," said my stepmom.

My girlfriend reached out and touched my shoulder. "I'm so confused," she said. "What's her name? How old is she?"

"I can't tell if you're joking," I said.

"She's joking," said my stepmom.

"I know your brother," said my girlfriend, "and your brother's girlfriend."

"Mark has a girlfriend?" My father looked around the table.

I shrugged. "News to me."

"Mia," said my girlfriend. "They've been together for years…"

"Mia's my sister," I said.

My girlfriend looked embarrassed, and I took her hand. "You're joking, right?" I whispered.

My girlfriend shook her head and said nothing else. She resumed eating slowly, her eyes creased. My father laughed once, sharply, and shrugged, and fed the toddler some quiche. From the kitchen, pots clanked and water ran. We ate without speaking for several minutes.

"Can we play with the dog?" the six-year-old asked.

The question made it seem like he was referring to a specific dog in the room, and briefly I looked around for it. "Olive died a long time ago," I said. "You remember her?"

The six-year-old nodded. "How did it die?"

I glanced at my father and my stepmom, their faces poised over their plates. "She got sick," I said.

"Sick how?"

"Sick in her...in her brain," I said. "Not sick, really. Confused. About whether people were her friends or not. And we couldn't make her better."

My girlfriend stood abruptly and disappeared into the kitchen. The baby in my stepmom's arms began to cry. "Oh, hush, hush, hush," my stepmom rubbed the baby's tummy. "Hush, hush, hush." The toddler in my father's lap, his mouth full of half-chewed quiche, scrunched up his face and cried along with the baby. My father ignored him, sawing a piece of bacon in half and forking it into his mouth. "Hush, hush, hush," said my stepmom. I rubbed my face with the heels of my palms. The six-year-old and the four-year-old bickered beside me. There was a crash in the kitchen, and my girlfriend's voice.

My stepmom called in Spanish into the den. A woman—heavyset with short, gray hair, dressed in teal scrubs—appeared at the doorway. She took the baby from my stepmom and disappeared back into the den.

"Let me tell you something," my father said at a normal register, as if there were not two babies crying. I leaned forward and strained to hear him, but most of what he said was swallowed up by the noise. "This whole...in," he said. "With this student and... could avoid all this if...real school...beyond help. There's nothing you...wasting your time...make a difference over...whatever you're doing. Go teach at a...kids have integrity...interested in learning, and... impact."

I nodded, and then shook my head. "I really don't know," I said. "Most of my students are so smart, and work so hard, and really inspire me in so many ways. A lot of these people are immigrants, parents, working full-time jobs on top of pursuing their degrees, and their commitment, their *integrity*, is astounding. I don't think they're beyond help at all. I think they're taking steps to live better lives, to create opportunities for themselves and their families. I'm honored to be part of that, to facilitate that in any way."

My father shrugged. "I can't hear you," he said, and sipped his coffee.

There was a flurry of movement beside me. The four-year-old recoiled and clutched her face. Her eyes widened and her mouth rippled, and she threw her head back and began to cry. The six-year-old blinked, a sheepish grin on his face.

"Did you just hit your sister?" my stepmom glared at the six-year-old. The six-year-old's eyes hopped around the table. "That's it," my stepmom said. "You're in a timeout when we get home."

"No," said the six-year-old. "No, I'm not." He looked at my father, who looked away. The six-year-old opened his mouth, closed it, and then he, too, started to cry.

"Well, I think that's our cue," my stepmom said, standing. "Four simultaneous crying babies are usually enough of a hint."

My father rose, threw one more piece of bacon into his mouth. "This is our exit music," he grinned.

My girlfriend appeared in the kitchen doorway. Her eyes were pink and there were dark splotches of water on her shirt. Her hands were balled into fists. "Everything okay in here?" she asked.

"We're gonna go," said my stepmom. "Everyone's getting a little salty."

"What a shame," said my girlfriend, though I perceived her shoulders relaxing, and her hands unclenched. "It was great to see you," she hugged my stepmom.

"Oh, Lamella," my stepmom called into the kitchen. "Thank you for a wonderful breakfast."

There was no response. Water ran. Dishes clanked.

"She's having trouble hearing these days," my girlfriend said.

My stepmom shrugged and ushered the crying children toward the door.

My father patted me on the back, balancing the grumpy toddler in his other arm. "Good luck," he said. "I say get out while you still can." He winked, and I winked back, unsure to what he was referring.

I saw everyone out while my girlfriend retreated into the kitchen. From the porch I watched my stepmom and the nurse place the children into a white SUV. I could still hear the children's atonal shrieks after the doors closed, and I waved as the car pulled away from the curb and lumbered off. I imagined them all in there, the children's sobs gradually waning to sniffles, maybe one or two of them falling asleep while the nurse, in the third-row seat with the baby and the toddler, gazed out the tinted windows at the quiet street, maybe thinking about home, or thinking about her own children if she had any. I imagined my father and stepmom talking in the front, one of them saying, "Well that was nice," and the other saying, "Yes, very pleasant," and the other, my father this time, saying, "I don't know. I worry about Mel," and my stepmom saying, "How come?" and my father saying, "He just doesn't seem to know what's going on. He's wandering through life," and my stepmom saying, "And that girlfriend of his. So moody. Very emotionally immature, both of them," and my father nodding in agreement, guiding the SUV toward the highway, heading south with the river on their right, back toward the city. And for most of the drive they don't talk, and the kids lull in the back, the nurse catching a few minutes of sleep herself, her head rocking back against the seat rest until the car hits a rut, then snapping up, checking the baby, looking out the window at the river, at the green hills and obscure structures on the far bank, my stepmom texting her friends from the passenger seat about how her stepson is a mess, is just wandering through life, and that he probably gets it from his mother, and that it's really pathetic, really pitiful, and her kids will *never* turn out like that, her kids will be successful and confident and thrive at whatever they set their minds to. And maybe she reaches out for my father's hand while he drives, though I doubted it, and imagined instead that they touch rarely, only to copulate, or else by accident, and I imagined my father pulling the car up in front of their building, and the doorman helping my stepmom and the nurse unload the kids, and then my father pulling the car around the corner to the garage, leaving it there, walking up the ramp into the afternoon sunlight, turning and heading in the opposite direction of the building, out into the city, blending into the throngs of pedestrians—going somewhere—and the further he goes the hazier he becomes, until he is impossible to imagine at all, one of millions of faceless people.

Back inside I found my girlfriend escorting the old woman by its arm from the kitchen to the den. The old woman took delicate, narrow steps. My girlfriend's lips were thin. "Lamella needs to rest," she said. "Will you finish cleaning up in the kitchen?"

"Of course," I said.

My girlfriend guided the old woman to the sofa and lowered it gingerly. Its papery skin dimpled beneath it, and it grimaced and croaked. My girlfriend arranged the pillows behind its head, and lifted its legs onto the cushions. "Your feet are so swollen," my girlfriend said, rubbing them gently, her brow furrowed and her hair unraveling from its bun and bowing around her face. She started to cry then, silently, the tears bleeding from her eyes and dropping onto the old woman's toes. The old woman, its holes sagging, raised a white, varicose hand and beckoned to my girlfriend, who laid her head on its lap. "Hush, hush," the old woman said, stroking her hair. My girlfriend's tears pooled in the ditches of the old woman's thigh.

I gathered a pile of dishes from the dining room table and carried them to the kitchen. Most of the mess had already been cleaned, and I rinsed the remaining plates and placed them in the dishwasher. I peeked back into the den, where my girlfriend cried silently, and the old woman petted her hair. "Hush," it wheezed. "Hush, hush, hush."

I felt exhausted. It was because I had overslept, I reasoned, and now I was out of whack. I slipped through the den, where it appeared that my girlfriend and the old woman were asleep, and stole upstairs to the bedroom. I shed my clothes and got into bed and immediately drifted off against the cool sheets. My thoughts tumbled and spilled and melded into strange, misshapen objects. Raspy voices and narrow faces and full lips that curled up at the edges. I picked up my phone and there was another e-mail from Samanta Sewenger:

'Dear Mel, I regret my tone earlier the truth is I am scared of how I feel about you and how bad I want you I know it is wrong yet I cannot stop thinking about you I want you I want you to take me and kiss me and hold me down and fuck me until I am dead.' My eyes startled open at the last syllable. The crack along the ceiling had worsened. I rolled onto my side and studied the fibers of the sheets as if through the lens of a microscope, and found they were so porous that there was more absence than substance, less sheet than sheet, and I awoke further, disturbed by the implications. I sat up and rolled my neck. My mouth was dry, and I balanced my way down the hall to the bathroom and drank from the faucet until water sloshed in my stomach. There was a voice downstairs, seething. "Useless..." it said. Or maybe it was, "You're foolish..." Or, "Toothless..." Or, "The truth is..." I crept down the stairs as quietly as I could, but my foot depressed a creaky step, and the voice stopped. My girlfriend appeared at the bottom and frowned as if she didn't recognize me. Her eyes flittered over my body, and I realized I'd forgotten to dress after napping. I dropped a hand to cover myself.

"What are you doing?" she said.

"I was just coming to get water," I said.

Her eyes narrowed, as if this seemed unlikely. I continued downstairs and sidled past her, and filled a glass with water in the kitchen, which I proceeded merely to hold. I was already so full of water that it roiled uncomfortably in my belly.

In the den, my girlfriend was standing over the sofa, looking down at the old woman. It was twisted on its side, its head dangling over its shoulder, its hands knotted as if in some great reluctance.

"Is everything okay?" I asked.

"She's dying," my girlfriend said.

I nodded slowly. "Should we call someone?"

My girlfriend scoffed. "Like who? Who can stop this?"

I drank from the glass, the kitchen water pattering into the bathroom water, and my stomach turned.

The old woman emitted a rattle and rolled onto its back. My girlfriend gasped. I tried to determine what had shocked her, but there was nothing different save that the holes in the old woman's face were baggier than before, and its white skin sagged off its body like a rumpled blanket. Its hair was patchy and its breath was staggered and faint. My girlfriend put her face in her hands and arched her back. I touched the back of her neck and she flinched. I set the glass on the coffee table and embraced her, kissed the top of her head.

"Hush, hush, hush," I said.

She looked up at me with pink, dry eyes. She pressed her mouth to mine roughly and sucked at my lips. Our teeth clanked. She snarled my hair in her fist, and cursed and kissed me so hard that my lip split against my teeth and I tasted iron. I tried to soothe her, to slow her, but she slapped my hands away and clutched at my jaw, and she tugged down her pants until they were bunched around her thighs. She bit my lip, splitting it again, and cursed and kneaded at me frantically, carelessly, and pushed me onto the sofa. My arm landed on the old woman's feet, and I withdrew it. My girlfriend tore her pants off one leg, so they dangled from the ankle of the other, and she fell on me and cursed again, and forced me inside her. She was dry and our skin rended. "Stop—wait," I said. But her eyes were clenched shut, as if with pain or concentration, and she thrust a hand against my head, turning it and straining it toward the old woman. Its eyes were gone, the holes in its face a convent of crypts receding into darkness, deeper than the width of its head—deeper even than the width of the sofa and the boundary of the floor and the pits of the earth. My girlfriend let go of my head and put her hand on the old woman's ankle for balance, and the old woman's body jostled as my girlfriend lurched. Pain stabbed through my penis, and I protested, begged her to slow down. But her face was knotted sharply, and my mouth twisted shut. I noticed my dark reflection in the television, my face ghoulish, and I closed my eyes.

Finally she clambered off me. I looked down at my lap, and my skin was raw and pink. My girlfriend trudged to the stairs, her pants dangling from her ankle as if she'd been in a terrible accident and now wandered, dazed, down the middle of the road. She lumbered up the stairs. I looked at the old woman. Its toothless, eyeless holes were dilated, as if to capture more light. It didn't appear to be breathing. I touched its leg. It was cold and dry.

My girlfriend reappeared, dressed in a new outfit. She threw a bundle of clothes at me. "Take care of this," she said.

"Take care of what?"

"*This!*" she struck the air in the direction of the old woman. "It was a mistake from the beginning. Thank god it's over." She tugged on a pair of boots.

"Where are you going?"

"Out," she said. "With a friend." She slid into a coat and snatched her purse off the knob on the hallway closet. "Just make sure it's gone by the time I get back." She left, flinging the front door shut behind her. I heard her car start, and the crackle of tires on gravel.

I held the bundle of clothes in my arms gingerly, as if they were breakable. Slowly I unbunched them and worked them over my body. They were complicated—there seemed to be too many holes in them—and it took me awhile to figure out where my arms and legs went, and where to stick my head. Once I was dressed, I stared blankly at the body, which appeared to shrink before my eyes. I churned out sluggish and preposterous ideas about what to do with it. I paced around the first floor of the house, my eyes scanning the furniture and the objects scattered about as if they might reveal to me—or better yet, *accomplish* for me—my task. In the kitchen I paused at the sliding doors and gazed out at the yard, at the rampart of bramble and at the tufted grass. I slid the doors open and stepped out into the cold. I turned and faced the house, which seemed a different shade of gray than I remembered. I regarded the oak tree that wrestled up from the house's edge, whose branches braided out across the plain sky. I traced the maze of trenches along its trunk. The 'S + L' engraved in it seemed to be higher up than it had earlier in the day, higher than the top of my head.

I continued around the side of the house to the small door under the porch, unlatched it, and groped around in the dark hole until I found what I was looking for and returned to the oak tree, my bare feet throbbing on the cold grass. I drove the shovel into the ground a few feet from the roots of the tree. The ground was dense and unyielding. I drove it again, and again, and slowly chipped away through the grass and into the dark soil beneath. I set the displaced soil in a clump among the roots of the tree, and as I dug I found that those same roots extended further and deeper than I'd expected. I had to hack through them and remove them from the hole in sections, which further belabored the already excruciating process. Soon, despite the cold, I was sweating and panting. I heard my girlfriend's voice: "Just make sure it's gone before I get back." I dug faster, feeling the seconds crank by, and the minutes dissolve into hours, and the sun lowered itself below the crests of the houses behind me and I cast a long shadow into the hole. I managed to dig a hole deep enough to submerge my legs up to my knees inside it, and about my width and half the length of my body.

I rested the shovel against the oak tree and went inside, the heat triggering an expulsion of sweat from my body that drenched my shirt and the front of my pants. In the den, the body had coiled around itself, its arms bent, the holes in its face yawning so widely apart that the flesh between them was stretched as thin as wire. I looked around for something to wrap it in, but there was nothing in the den. I went to the bedroom and grabbed the first thing I saw—the puce dress my girlfriend had worn to dinner last night, which was draped over the foot of the bed—and I took the red shoebox from beneath the bedside table, which jangled as I descended the stairs. I covered the body with the dress, wrapping it tightly, and I lifted it —it was appallingly light, the dress itself seeming to weigh more—placed it over my shoulder, and carried it and the shoebox outside. The air was sallow and my sweat-soaked shirt stiffened in the cold. I lowered the body into the hole, folding it down into the hard dirt. In the pale air, the dress looked red. I opened the shoebox and poured the teeth—there were only seven or eight of them—over the body, and set the box aside. I used the shovel to reset the dirt into the hole. And finally, just as the last wisps of light retreated below the horizon, I regarded the dark, damp mound of dirt. I left the shovel leaning against the tree, and I went inside.

I set the empty shoebox on the dining room table and went upstairs and climbed into the shower. I squatted there, too exhausted to wash myself, trusting the water and gravity to clean me. The water spiraled into the holes in the drain, and I started to remember something, something important that I had reminded myself not to forget. But it dissolved before it revealed itself to me. I crawled from the shower and dried myself, and went down the hall to the bedroom, shutting the door to the study as I passed it. I got into the bed and as I lay there I thought about my mom—and I missed her terribly in that moment, and I needed her. I picked up my phone from the bedside table and called her, but it rang through, and I barely managed to set my phone down again before sleep overtook me. I dreamt only of being enveloped in darkness for many hours, until light bled in from the edges and morning arrived. I was alone in the bed. I dressed and went downstairs. My girlfriend was asleep on the sofa, carved in slats of light that sliced through the blinds. She wore the same clothes she'd left the house in. I forewent making coffee, gathered my things, left the house quietly, and drove to work.

There was a high-pitched whistling as I drove. I could not figure out where it was coming from, because the windows were all the way up, and it did not sound like it was coming from the engine but rather from inside the car. Eventually it grew so grating that I rolled down the windows to drown it out, though soon I started to shiver so I rolled them back up, and the whistling resumed.

I parked on campus and watched the earliest students saunter to class. I thought about my own students, some of whom were as old as my parents and had children of their own. Just now, late in their lives, they were returning to school to pursue some dream that had too long languished under the floorboards of their obligations. I thought about my mom, and remembered that I had called her last night, half asleep, and I tried to remember what we had talked about. But all I could remember was the sound of her voice. I checked my phone and saw that the outgoing call had lasted only thirty seconds, and remembered that she had not picked up. I tried to figure out what conversation I was remembering, and decided it was just a confused amalgamation of all the conversations I'd ever had with my mom in my life. My thumb hovered over the phone, but I could not decide what I would say to her if she picked up now, or what I had wanted to say last night. I left the car and headed toward the café for a coffee. I paused on the way and texted my girlfriend, 'I love you.' I walked a few more paces, paused again, and texted, 'I'm sorry.' A pair of girls passed me, glancing back as they did, and I recognized them as students of mine, though I could not remember their names, nor which class they'd been in. I squeezed a smile at them that felt like a grimace, and they hurried along. I heard them laughing behind me, and I wondered if they were laughing at me or at something else, or if it was them laughing at all.

I arrived at the classroom and took my place at the front of the room while students trickled in. Once everyone was there, I returned their latest papers. I was left with only one unreturned paper—by a student named Stephen whose face I could not recall —which I put in my bag. I described their next writing assignment and went over some strategies for approaching it. Class ended quickly, and the students filed out of the room. I waited at my desk in case anyone had any questions or wanted to talk, though no one approached. Alone in the classroom, I stared into one of the corners as if at something slowly materializing there, and was only interrupted when a group of students entered for the next class. I gathered my things and left.

I checked my phone in the stairwell. My girlfriend had not responded. I wondered what she could have done the night before to make her so tired, or why she had slept downstairs on the sofa. I had an e-mail from Dean Oresco, requesting that I visit her office as soon as I was able. I hurried down the stairs, out the side exit, and cut across the grass up the hill toward the administration building. I announced myself to the woman at the front desk—a different woman from the one last week, with short gray hair and an angular jaw—who told me to go ahead in, that the dean was expecting me. On my way from the desk to the office door I thought suddenly of Samanta Sewenger. My chest tightened. There was not enough time to prepare myself for what I would say or how I would act when I saw her. When I entered, I found Dean Oresco alone. She stood and extended her hand to me.

"Thank you for coming in," she said.

I nodded and sat.

"How was your weekend?" she asked.

"Uneventful," I said.

"Good, good." She moved a folder from one end of the desk to the other. Behind her, through the window, students moved silently down paths. Blemishes of gray snow marked the grass. There was a row of books along the windowsill, bracketed between two white bookends in the shape of two girls' profiles. Dean Oresco was saying something.

"I'm sorry?" I said.

"You're growing a beard," she repeated, stroking her own chin as if to indicate where a beard might go.

"Not deliberately," I said.

"Well, it suits you," she smiled.

"I got your e-mail," I said. "Which is why I'm here."

"We're just waiting for Samanta," Dean Oresco sat back in her chair. "She should be here any second."

My eyes flickered to the door at the side of the room. I breathed slowly. There was a smell of burning wood, and faintly of leather, and of Dean Oresco's floral perfume. I concentrated on the concatenation of these smells, which roiled together into something richly organic. I was struck at once by a string of words, a sentence that fashioned itself to me and hung there in my mind. I slid my phone from my pocket and wrote it down, and I looked at it, and I felt something stir in me, something long forgotten. I felt the impulse to write another sentence, and perhaps another after that. I crossed my legs and felt blood rush through me.

The phone on Dean Oresco's desk rang. "Excuse me," she said to me as she answered it. "Yes? Okay... Oh no...Oh...I'm so sorry to hear...I'll call her this afternoon...yes, thank you, Tina." She set the phone down and blinked. "Samanta won't be joining us," she said. "There was a death in her family and she's had to catch a plane back home. Texas, I think..."

Something untangled in me. "That's terrible," I said. "I'm sorry to hear."

Dean Oresco nodded and shrugged. "She's a lovely girl. So far from home. Meanwhile, I suppose you and I can talk. It won't be a long conversation—I have another meeting in fifteen minutes."

I folded my hands in my lap.

"So, we've reviewed the accusation," she said. "The paper in question and the previous papers that Mister Jones submitted to you. We also looked at some of his writing from other classes. And we've decided, beyond any doubt, that he did not write this latest paper. And we appreciate you bringing it to our attention."

I nodded slowly, absorbing this. "Okay," I said.

"Carl Jones has been contacted, and he will no longer be returning to the school. And we want to apologize to you for all this...Though of course in the future, if you encounter the issue again, it is protocol to notify the administration about your suspicion *before* you inform the student."

"Of course," I said, and through the window a cloud rushed across the sun, dampening the air briefly, and when the light reemerged it felt different, and I thought of my girlfriend.

"Anyway, that's really it," Dean Oresco leaned forward. "Again, we apologize. But you need to appreciate that we take these things seriously, both as a means of protecting our students *and* of protecting the integrity and reputations of our faculty."

"I appreciate all of that," I said. "And I appreciate your time, and the seriousness with which you took this matter. I'm glad it's resolved."

Dean Oresco nodded. "Before you go," she said, picking up a red folder from across her desk. "I want to tell you about a full-time faculty position that's opening in the English department. It's a tenure track position—or the equivalent of a tenure track position here—and I think you might be well suited for it, seeing as you've been with us now for some time, and you are well liked by your students, and by your colleagues." She handed the red folder across the desk. "We'll be sending out a general announcement about the position next week, but I thought you might want a head start. If you're interested, of course."

I took the folder. It was light, as if empty. "Yes," I said. "Thank you."

"Don't worry too much about the application," she said. "Just return it to me once you've filled out the important parts. We'd like to see you become a more permanent member of our school, and to see you rewarded for your hard work."

I slid the folder into my bag. "I would like that too."

"Good," Dean Oresco said. "Now I have what is destined to be a very long and pointless meeting across campus. But please be in touch about the position. The good offices go quick, and we don't want you getting stuck in the basement."

"I will," I stood, and Dean Oresco stood, and we shook hands.

"Oh, and of course you are welcome to resume your English 101 class," she said. "I know your students will be happy to have you back."

"That's great," I said as an inexplicable pang of regret tightened and then released in my chest.

I nodded to the woman at the desk, who smiled back, and I bought another coffee on my way across campus to teach 101. As my students arrived, I made a point to greet each one individually. Once everyone was there, I asked them what they wanted to do for their final projects. An essay? A presentation? Did they want to work in groups? We tossed around ideas, some of which were solid, and ambitious. I asked them to write up a project proposal and bring it to class on Wednesday. I stressed that I really wanted them to have fun with this, to pick topics that interested them. Ultimately, I explained, this was *their* time. Not mine, not the school's. This was for them. It was their opportunity, to learn and grow and widen their understandings of the world, to have fuller, more profound experiences in their lives. I gave myself a chill as I spoke, and I thought I detected some bristling, some nodding from my students. I dismissed them twenty minutes early on the condition that they enjoy the day. As they were leaving, one of them—who last week had dozens of piercings in her face that were now missing, so that her face was speckled with tiny holes—approached me.

"Would you be able to write a letter of recommendation for me," she asked. "For my transfer essay to NYU?"

I leaned on the desk, which groaned beneath me. "Of course," I said. "I'm glad you asked me, Michelle."

She started to say something, then stopped.

"Just e-mail me the link to wherever it needs to be submitted," I said.

"It's due on Tuesday."

"You mean tomorrow?"

She nodded.

"Okay, well…Look. I'll do the best I can for you, but it's not a lot of time, and I can't promise it will be as good as it would have been if you'd given me more notice."

She nodded.

"So send me that link as soon as you can, and I'll take care of it."

"Thank you," she said, hiking up her backpack as she left.

I was proud of her for taking the initiative to transfer to a good school, and proud of myself for being approachable enough that she would ask for my help. I gathered my things and started to leave when I noticed someone sitting in the corner by the window, slumped over a desk. "Everything okay?" I asked. They did not stir. I approached, glancing back over my shoulder at the door and the otherwise empty classroom. When I was a few paces away I scoffed and laughed. It was not a person at all, just someone's coat and backpack left in such a position as to connote, vaguely, the shape of a body.

I made my way across campus. I thought about Carl Jones as I passed the Student Center. The sun bored through the medium height of the sky, flooding my eyes with light. Just last week he and his friends had threatened me, right here on this section of path. It served him right to be expelled, because he was a real piece of shit. I hoped his experience taught him about consequences and gave him pause in the future. The truth was I didn't hate him, but just felt bad for him. He didn't know any better. I was proud of myself for being so understanding, so empathetic. I wished Carl Jones all the best. I told myself I wished there was more I could have done for him.

I drove home with the windows down. It had warmed nicely through the afternoon, and I savored the crisp air that roared into the car and drowned the voices on the radio into a muffled belch of consonants. I parked behind my girlfriend's car, and inside I found her on the sofa, packets and folders strewn on the coffee table.

"Hey," she said.

"Hey." I set my bag down and sat beside her. "How are you?"

"Looking at some options for massage school," she said, indicating the table.

"That's fantastic," I said.

"How was your day?"

"It was great. They expelled that guy."

"That's good."

"Yeah. And then, probably because they felt bad for dragging me through the mud, they offered me a full-time position."

"That's amazing, love." My girlfriend put her hand on my knee.

"I'll be making three, four times what I make now. And I can help you pay for school, wherever you decide to go."

She lifted one of the packets, which showed a serene, topless woman lying on her stomach, a pair of disembodied hands kneading the skin on her back. "Some of these are very expensive," she said.

"It's worth it," I said. "If it's what you want to do, if it'll make you happy."

She pursed her lips. "I'm sorry about last night," she said.

"What do you mean?"

"I got home late and didn't feel like going to bed yet, so I sat down here to watch television and fell asleep. I just don't want you thinking I was, like, avoiding you or something."

"That's okay," I put my hand on the back of her neck. "I figured that's what happened. Did you have fun with your friends?"

She shrugged. "I guess. I don't know. I'm kind of over going to bars and stuff. I want to focus. I want to further myself."

"I support that."

My girlfriend leaned back. "We're really doing this."

"Mm-hm."

"Sometimes it hits me," she said. "Part of me, I think, is stuck in this place of being a child. And occasionally it gets through that I'm not, that I'm almost thirty. And it's scary and weird. Like, it happened too fast."

I remembered something then. "Do you want to take a drive?"

"Where?"

"I want to get my books out of storage, put them back in my study."

"Sure."

"I'm thinking about, I don't know, maybe trying to write something," I said.

"I think you should."

I studied our reflections in the dark television, where it was difficult to tell us apart. Outside, a car rumbled down the street, and a voice shouted. But it had nothing to do with us in here.

"Do you want to get married?" I asked.

She looked at me as if she had not understood, and she smiled faintly, but as if to someone else, and took my hand. "Let's take one thing at a time," she said. "We're still so young."

We left the house and got in the car. I could smell the floral soapiness of her hair as I backed the car out of the driveway. She turned up the radio and reclined in her seat, stretching her strong legs on the dashboard. I reached out and touched her, briefly, and in the low winter sun her skin glowed golden, and her hair was dark.

About the Author

Max Halper grew up in New York City and now lives upstate. Lamella is his first book.

About the Artist

Dolce Paganne (a.k.a Ceren Aksungur) is an artist based in Istanbul and Brussels. Her surreal paintings are featured worldwide in leading art magazines such as Hi Fructose and Beautiful Bizarre and exhibited in galleries & museums in the USA, UK, Italy, France, Turkey, Belgium, Germany, Australia.

Follow her on Instagram (@dolce_paganne) and Twitter (@DolcePaganne).

Dark Stories for Dark Minds

BAD DREAM
ENTERTAINMENT

www.BadDreamEntertainment.com
www.Facebook.com/BadDreamEntertainment
www.Twitter.com/BadDreamPub